STEALING KISSES

BOOK 6

VIRGINIA'DELE SMITH

Books are Ubiquitous

Published by Books are Ubiquitous, Inc.
in the United States of America
booksareubiquitous.com

Books are Ubiquitous is a federally registered trademark.

This book is a work of fiction.

Names, characters, places, and incidents either are the product of the author's imagination or are used fictitiously. Any resemblance to actual persons, living or dead, business establishments, events, or locales is entirely coincidental.

Paperback ISBN: 978-1-957036-24-3

———

Titles by Virginia'dele Smith

Sadie & Sam: PART 1 - Introductory Short Story (FREE)
Book 0: My Manifesto - Short Memoir (FREE)

The Davenports
Book 1: Grocery Girl
Book 2: In the Trenches
Book 3: Three Times to Make Sure
Book 4: Take a Chance on Love
The Davenports EAT — A Green Hills Cookbook

Book 5: *Undeveloped Love*
A Christmas Collection Novella

Book 6: *Stealing Kisses*
A Valentine's Sweetheart Story

Book 7: *Phoebe* (coming soon)
The Prairie Roses Collection

VALENTINE'S SWEETHEARTS

The *Valentine's Sweethearts* series is a collection
of 18 heartwarming clean romance stories
as sweet as a box of chocolates.

Featuring popular tropes such as fake dating, friends to lovers,
opposites attract, grumpy/sunshine, accidental marriages, love
at first sight, there's something for every romantic in the series
and so much more!

Fate brings together couples who discover
that true connection goes beyond sweet nothings printed on
candy. And as they navigate the season of love and their own
hesitations, they learn that sometimes, all it takes is one
heartfelt message to change everything.

***Check out every book in the
Valentine's Sweethearts Series!
Available on Amazon.***

To my writing tribe:

Kathryn Mykel
Jan Mau Hill
Evans Kaye
MJ Krause-Chivers
Violet Batejan

Without your daily encouragement
and accountability,
I'd have run for the hills a thousand times!
Instead, with your love and support,
I'm seven books in with no end in sight.
Thank you, sweet friends 🩶

1

———

"...thy heart is ever harder than stone."
Telemachus to his mother, Penelope
The Odyssey by Homer, Book 23

Sunday, February 7, 2021

Remarkable blessings exist in unison with proportional burdens.

On a Sunday afternoon in early February, Baylin O'Casey embraced both her blessings and her burdens as she rode her horse across the most beautiful land in all the world: a breathtaking combination of flat fields, rolling plains, creeks and streams, tall pines, and rounded oaks. Located just outside Green Hills, Oklahoma, all six hundred thirty-three acres of fertile ground had belonged to her family for the past hundred twenty-five years.

She woke well before dawn each day, allowing Baylin a front-row seat to experience the soft, gradual transition from dark to light as the morning sun rose over the hay field; if she slept any longer, she'd run out of hours well before she ran out of chores. The chickens further entertained Baylin, chatting amongst themselves and clucking at her in a feeding frenzy when she tossed out their breakfast and gathered their eggs each day. Checking water troughs, spreading hay and straw, feeding the rest of the animals…those jobs fell to Baylin as well. Hired hands helped — to the extent the farm could afford — but without full-time employees, the bulk of the operation and most of the chores sat heavy on Baylin's shoulders.

She faced this reality with a gracious heart…because losing the land or closing the farm business would've broken it. Growing crops, tending animals, and managing the house brought with them purpose and stability. Her staunch determination guaranteed their O'Casey Farm legacy lived on.

At least once a week, Baylin rode fence lines to check for breaks or needed repairs. From her tall perch astride her horse, Baylin could see to the ends of the earth.

"Ah, Penelope," she said, leaning down to rub the horse's neck as they cantered over lush winter grass. "It's another gorgeous day."

Despite a cool, crisp morning, Baylin tugged her beanie from her head, shaking out her long, golden-red hair and lifting her face to absorb the sun's strong, bright rays.

Life was good and Baylin was content.

Hard work exhausted her mind and body, and the various hobbies she enjoyed fed her need to be creative.

Since taking on full responsibility for running the farm a few years earlier, those creative endeavors had blossomed into full-fledged side gigs. Those side gigs had developed into profitable streams of revenue for the farm, even if those sideline businesses sometimes added a multitude of tasks to her already full plate.

February meant Green Hills' annual Sweetheart Festival, and Baylin had a million things to do before it began in just a few short days.

She reviewed her to-do list in her mind while surveying the fence line, the fields, and the other animals out grazing. Everything the light touched belonged to Baylin…

Except one thing, something red and shiny off in the distance.

"Is that a car?" she wondered aloud. Penelope nickered in response. "I *sooo* do not have time for that to be a car — or a human — all the way out here."

Baylin nudged Penelope into a gallop with a continuous prayer looping in her mind: *Please don't be a car.*

She stood in the stirrups to see better as they flew over the earth.

Definitely a car, and definitely a human.

"Splendid," she grumbled.

Baylin's day took a deep dive for the worse.

2

———

***Surprise is the greatest gift
which life can grant us.
Boris Pasternak***

"That hunk of junk yours?" asked the beautiful woman riding the magnificent horse.

"I sure wouldn't call a 1955 Porsche 550 Spyder a hunk of junk," Teddy Gwenn answered with a gleeful guffaw.

The fiery princess had the warmth of an iceberg, which did nothing to diminish her magnificence. Her perch upon the massive beast and the way she looked down her pert little nose at him — a mere peasant in her realm — should've been off-putting. Instead, her disdain delighted Teddy, nearly to the point of jubilation.

Coach Hayes, Teddy's mentor throughout high school and college, had always claimed Teddy was half fool and fifty percent crazy. The woman lording over him in that moment might prove the irascible old man right.

"But, yeah, she's mine," he continued, allowing a shy grin while shrugging with pride.

Back in the second grade, Teddy earned a door prize ticket at the elementary school book fair. He'd never purchased anything at the annual library event, but he had eyed the books, the toys, and the trinkets plenty. As the principal drew tickets from the box and read students' names aloud to the assembly, Teddy scrunched his eyes, hoping and praying for a copy of Dav Pilkey's *Captain Underpants and the Preposterous Plight of the Purple Potty People* book... Honestly, any *Captain Underpants* would have been terrific. Teddy had read every one of them, checked them out of the library multiple times, and wanted one of his own *real bad*. When he heard his name, Teddy jumped with a whoop, elated to receive a book. Winding through the other kids, he hustled to the front of the cafeteria wearing an ear-splitting smile.

I won. I really won!

When he got to the stage, though, the librarian handed him a plastic bag encasing a rolled-up piece of paper. A poster? He'd won some dumb poster when all he'd wanted was a new book. But he took the poster home all the same, unrolling it to reveal a sleek, cherry red sports car. Not just a sports car, but a vintage racing model that sat close to the ground with a weathered covered bridge in the background, the rough road and soft green grass along the bar ditch juxtaposed with the car's expensive-looking shiny interior and spotless exterior. The waxed tires, sleek and low profile with silky smooth aluminum rims, reflected light almost as vividly as the paint dazzled in the sun's bright rays.

Teddy had decided the poster was pretty cool, even if it wasn't *Captain Underpants*. He taped it to the dingy wall in his room, and he'd come to love it. Over the years, the poster transformed into a talisman, a tangible source of motivation.

No matter where their family moved, the poster went with Teddy... No matter how challenging the days, how long and cold the nights, or how heartbreaking the defeats, the poster provided constant encouragement.

He took the poster to Louisiana State University, hanging it in his dorm room, despite the teasing and ribbing he received from his teammates and friends. After Atlanta drafted him in the fifteenth round, the poster traveled with him through the minor leagues…first in Rome, Georgia, then to Pearl, Mississippi during Teddy's stint with the Double A Braves, and on to Lawrenceville, Georgia and the Gwinnett Stripers for two short stays at the Triple A level.

When the Atlanta Braves called him up to the big league, Teddy's first purchase had been to get that old poster custom framed to hang it in a place of prominence…in the garage of *his* home, which had been his second significant purchase…one bought and paid for, one nobody would ever take away.

After a record-setting rookie season led to a new, rather hefty contract with the Braves, Teddy splurged for a third milestone purchase: the car. Not a replica, not a kit. *The* car, the one he'd promised himself to see in person with his own two eyes, the one he'd hoped to sit in some day, the one he'd prayed a million times he'd have a chance to drive before he died an old man…the one he parked right in front of his poster when he got home — *home* — after long hours of practice, after games just a few miles up the road at Truist Park, after series on the road, and after holidays with family and friends.

Teddy had also vowed to drive country roads, taking time to enjoy the journey of life, not only the destination, every opportunity he found. He'd never had a single problem with the car…until ten minutes earlier that day, when it had sputtered, slowed, and died next to a hay field in the middle of *Nowhere, Oklahoma.*

Teddy eyed his sweet sports car in consternation. What did fate hope to accomplish, conspiring to dump him at the feet of a veritable vixen? He rubbed a hand on the back of his neck as he turned toward the woman and her horse. After a moment's deliberation, he shrugged and began walking to close the distance between them. "I don't know what could've hap—"

"Wrong way," she interrupted, backing up the horse and gesturing to the asphalt behind Teddy with a jerk of her chin.

"I'm sorry?" He'd just been winding up to share his thoughts on what might've caused the engine to sputter and die without warning. The auburn-haired angel didn't care.

"You're walking the wrong way…town's in the other direction." With that, she reined the horse in a half circle and started off down the fence line.

"How far?" Teddy called out before she could get out of earshot.

She circled back to face Teddy but stopped again at least twenty yards away. He half-jogged closer.

Her eyes narrowed.

He halted. "*Exactly* how far is the walk to town?"

With cool composure, her gaze traveled from his face to his feet and back again. Her head tilted in consideration.

Did she like what she saw?

Teddy's heart sped up as she assessed him.

He'd never wanted to measure up as much as he wanted to right then.

Granted, his faded blue jeans had seen better days and were a bit thread-bare at the knees. Probably not the best first impression.

And for the drive, he'd thrown on his most comfortable, most broken-in pair of goat-skin Tecovas. His cowboy boots had started out a handsome golden brown that resembled a glass of aged scotch; years later, a healthy dose of scuffs and scrapes added personality. Perhaps also not what he'd have chosen if he'd known he'd be hoping to impress someone that day.

At least his shirt was a winner. Made from the softest cotton he'd ever felt, the t-shirt featured a cartoon peach wearing white baseball pants, a ball cap, and a cheesy smile standing with his chest puffed out in a round frame that read *Columbus Clingstones* across the chest of the long-sleeved, heather-orange tee. No one could find fault with the coolest team logo in all of minor league baseball.

When her eyes made their way from scuffed boot to threadbare jeans, across the awesome t-shirt, and back to his face, Teddy plastered on a confident grin. Little Orphan Annie did say, *You're never fully dressed without a smile.*

"You can make it in an hour…maybe a little less," the redhead in front of him announced.

Was that good or bad? Did it mean she'd found him strong and able? Or feeble and wanting?

I'm a professional athlete, for Pete's sake.

Glancing down at his feet, trying once more to see himself through her eyes, he laughed at his desire to know *her* thoughts. Just then, the sound of hooves clopping into the distance signaled that the object of his thoughts had left.

"You could give me a ride," he hollered after her, into the vacant space where the Titian goddess had been seconds before.

She didn't respond, just kept riding off into the sunset.

Teddy didn't move, admiring horse and rider until they disappeared into the horizon.

Then he followed them.

Twenty minutes later, a break in the pasture revealed a road and an open gate. A metal sign over a cattle guard announced Teddy had arrived at *O'Casey Farm.* The name fit. The feisty lass had to be an O'Casey.

Teddy followed the road until he came upon a sprawling farmhouse. An explosion of flower beds, shrubs, colorful planters, and winter flowers offered a much warmer welcome than had the cool queen, whom he suspected ruled the land with a fierce fist.

No one answered when he knocked on the front door, so he meandered around the wide front porch, complete with wooden rocking chairs, inviting pillows, and even a soft, well-used quilt folded across the railing. He continued to the side yard, where the red-headed beauty sat on her knees among tall green stalks. Whistling to announce his arrival, Teddy approached with caution. When he'd reached where she was extracting vegetables from the ground, he peered over her shoulder.

"Potatoes?" Teddy wondered aloud.

"You're more lost than you were before," she said by way of greeting, without even sparing him a quick glance.

"With such warm and fuzzy welcoming vibes, I couldn't help but see where you were headed." A happy-go-lucky smile accompanied his rebuttal.

She flashed him a glare of pure irritation.

Instead of rising to her bait, Teddy crouched beside her. He paid attention to what she was doing and how she did it, and then he began digging in the dirt, replicating her task.

"I got one," he exclaimed a few minutes later, raising his find in the air with a punch of victory.

She didn't congratulate Teddy, but she did grin…well, it was almost a grin…just a tiny bit of a change in the pursing of her lips, but he saw it. And it sparked a hum in his chest.

They worked in silence— well, *relative* silence, since Teddy hummed or whistled all the while.

When they'd made several piles of potatoes, Teddy's new fascination stood up, whisked the dirt from her hands and jeans, and walked into a shed on the far end of the garden. She returned with four wooden crates.

She filled a crate with the potatoes they'd already unearthed. Teddy followed her lead and filled a second crate.

Then she dug for more potatoes, so Teddy rooted around the soil for more potatoes, too.

Again, the enigmatic woman said nothing. To balance her silence, Teddy filled the space with a steady stream of upbeat whistles and hums.

On numerous occasions, Coach Hayes had also commented, often in exasperation, that he had never known a person to have a song in his heart 24/7 until he'd met Teddy; Coach vowed he wouldn't mind going back to that quieter time. But Coach never meant it. And Teddy never took offense; good vibes weren't meant to be tamped down. No, those set on grumpiness and frowns, cantankerous old coaches and stunning new strangers alike, challenged Teddy. Their crankiness became a gauntlet, daring Teddy to step up his game; their behavior inspired him to be more joyful, more vocal, and more playful until he got a reaction.

In the garden, Teddy and his reluctant leader didn't stop harvesting the vegetables until all four boxes threatened to overflow with a colorful array of gold, red, brown, and purple potatoes.

With the wooden crates too full to fit another potato, their digging was done.

"Are all these for us?" Teddy asked.

She flashed a smirk of disdain in his direction, exactly like the one she'd used upon his arrival in her garden.

"I mean, I love meat and potatoes, but that's a lot of potatoes!" he explained.

"There is no *us*. These are for the produce stand I'll have this weekend at the Sweetheart Festival." It was the most forthcoming she'd been in hours.

She stood and dusted off her jeans. Teddy stood and wiped his dirty hands on his pants, too. When she gathered trowels, he picked up the rest of the hand tools. When she bent to pick up a crate, Teddy intervened.

"I'll get those," he announced, stepping between her and her heavy boxes of vegetables. "Just show me where to go."

"I already tried that," she said with a sardonic glare. "It didn't work," she reminded him. Then she stepped around him, hefting a box that had to weigh fifty or sixty pounds.

"Huh," he huffed, but followed his ignoble grunt with what he'd been told was his most charming grin.

"Fine," she acquiesced. "Grab one and follow me. They go in the shed."

Teddy wanted to argue that he'd grab them all, but something said he'd be wasting his breath. Instead, he carried the fullest, heaviest-looking crate into the small building.

There Teddy discovered shelf after shelf full of the wooden crates. Almost every one of them overflowed with winter's harvest.

"Wow!" Teddy whistled to convey his approval. "This is quite a bounty. I had no idea so many vegetables grew in the cold."

And there it was again: her pursed-lip, head-shaking glance of derision, establishing his ignorance and stupidity without an ounce of filter. Gorgeous!

The fact that she didn't soften the blow to his ego warmed his heart like no team groupie — with their revealing outfits, over-painted faces, and simpering smiles — could.

Teddy made two more trips to carry in the rest of the potatoes. Then he snooped around the garden shed, nosying into buckets and bins, while his hostess organized shelves and jotted notes on a legal pad of yellow paper.

"I can't remember the last time I bought fresh produce at the store," Teddy admitted, picking up a cluster of green onions and inhaling their sharp, earthy scent.

"Probably wasn't all that fresh if it came from the store." Then she walked to the door, pausing at the threshold to glance at him over her shoulder. "Come on; I suppose you've earned dinner." She returned to the wall of crops she'd produced, picked up one of this and two of that. "You can see what fresh vegetables *actually* taste like," she added as she passed Teddy, flipped off the light, and left him standing in the dark.

3

Twenty Questions
Noun, plural but singular in construction ~
A game in which one player or team
tries to determine
from yes and no answers to
not more than 20 questions
what word or object the others
have chosen to be guessed

aylin placed a variety of squash, onions, and potatoes on the countertop beside the single basin ceramic sink. She turned the faucet to warm and began washing her hands, using a small bristle brush around and under her nails.

Her unwanted guest sidled up beside her and did the same.

She cast a withering glance his way. Once again, he seemed immune to her normally proficient stink-eye.

Instead of drying her hands, she began washing the vegetables she'd brought in for dinner. Again, and without asking permission, he copied her actions move for move.

Standing shoulder to shoulder, his tall, hulking body radiated more heat than the small kitchen could handle. Well, at least more heat than Baylin could handle.

To be fair, he wasn't *hulkish*, but he appeared too strong and too stout for comfort.

And too pretty.

Those eyes…the color of soft leafy greens, lighter than romaine but darker than cabbage. Baylin struggled not to stare in an effort to define their exact shade.

And the hair! What person not styled by a professional on a Hollywood set had that perfect swoopy thing going? He'd been driving a convertible! No one's hair looked good — and never *great* — after the wind blew through it for hours on end.

Baylin refused to acknowledge his stubbled beard, thick eyebrows, and light plum lips. They weren't worth considering…because no man should be so attractive.

Baylin left Mr. Perfect Body at the sink, assuming him capable of scrubbing vegetables without her assistance. She gathered the cast-iron skillet from the range, a cutting board from a bottom cabinet, and slid her chef's knife from its storage block. Setting up her station a healthy distance from the stranger in her kitchen, Baylin began slicing the squash he'd finished rinsing.

"Do you have a name?" she asked, careful not to sound the least bit interested in his answer.

He responded with another exuberant smile. Did the shining gleam in his eyes ever turn off?

"Theodore Robinson Gwenn," he replied. "But the whole world calls me Teddy."

"Well, Teddy, after dinner I'll drive you into town. Then you can be on your way."

Theodore-Call-Me-Teddy didn't get the hint.

As short-tempered and brusque as she'd tried to be all afternoon and evening, her demeanor had done zilch to diminish his good mood or inspire him to leave.

Teddy had hummed and chattered while they worked. Then he'd chattered and hummed some more while she cooked.

Baylin used all her energy to adjust to his presence, to the way he filled her farmhouse kitchen with natural ease. She worked hard to ignore the way Teddy's being there transformed the space back to the way it felt before Papa Joe's accident and before Grandma had needed round-the-clock dementia care.

Baylin's parents hated the farm, had never spent much time there, so she was alone in the house most of the time. And that suited her just fine.

She didn't have time for beautiful boys driving flashy cars... boys who drove those hot rods right out of Green Hills with the same careless speed that had brought them into town. Baylin didn't need complications, didn't have room to add one more time-consuming, energy-zapping item to her to-do list. The farm filled her days, quilting and reading and canning filled her evenings, and her friends and community filled her heart.

Essentially, life was perfect.

And that's how she intended for it to stay.

"And what can I call you?" Teddy asked, shaking Baylin from her wayward, some might say *prickly*, thoughts. "Just until you abandon me in town, of course. Without a place to stay. And no transportation. No friends...or even a—"

"Baylin," she interrupted. "I'm Baylin O'Casey."

Why had her voice come out that way? All deep and breathy? Good heavens, what was wrong with her?

Get a grip! He's here today, gone in five minutes.

"Baylin O'Casey," Teddy said with a glint of appreciation sparkling in his gorgeous green eyes. "It's a pleasure to meet you." He extended his hand to shake hers, and for a split second, a vision of him yanking her off a cliff into a free fall over a cavernous abyss flashed through her mind.

Baylin shook off that thought, too, reprimanding herself for being a silly fool. Since when had a random passer-through made her doubt herself? Never, that was when! And this wanderer wasn't about to be the first.

But when her palm met his, in what was supposed to be an innocent handshake, the zing of sensation that zapped through her hand and up her arm straight into her chest belied her certainty.

Baylin yanked back her hand and busied herself by sliding the chopped veggies into the skillet, drizzling olive oil over them, and adding seasonings to the pan. She lit the gas burner, stirred the mixture, and laid the lid on the skillet at a slight angle to let steam escape.

Teddy watched her like a hawk.

She refused to be unnerved.

When she took a leftover ham from the fridge and began cutting thick slices of the meat, Teddy helped himself to a scavenger hunt through her cabinets.

Seeming to find what he'd been looking for, Teddy set her small kitchen table with two plates, two napkins, and two sets of silverware.

Baylin had gotten in the bad habit of eating at her desk in the library, working on her computer between bites. The place settings, positioned with exacting care, looked strange. The pairs of everything felt too homey, too intimate. But also inviting…and nice.

"Can I steal a glass of milk? Or two?" Teddy asked after he'd located the tall, clear glasses in the upper cabinet by the refrigerator.

"Sure," Baylin allowed. "There's more where it came from," she added, making a slight attempt at conversation. She should've known better.

"Is it from your farm?" he asked. And he didn't come up for air until dinner was done, the dishes washed, and the kitchen spotless…

"So you have a real live dairy cow?" he marveled.

"I do," she confirmed.

"And a poor little pig died for us to have this ham?" Teddy didn't sound the least bit offended by the prospect as he piled multiple bites on his fork and devoured another slice.

"That he did," Baylin affirmed.

"All those vegetables in the garden shed are for the Sweetheart Festival?"

"Not all, but most."

"Why not all?

"Because I have to eat for the foreseeable future."

"That's fair," he agreed.

She only lifted an eyebrow in response.

"So, the Valentine's fair is a big deal?" Teddy asked.

"It is."

"And you're going to be working, selling your produce, the entire time it's going on?"

"I am."

"At a table?"

"I've rented booth space."

"That's cool."

"Thank you?" Baylin's reply came out like a question because really… What was he getting at?

"And you have to man the booth?"

"I do."

"The whole time?"

"Pretty much," she answered.

"But not every second?"

"No, not *every* second."

"What does it take to have a produce booth?"

"Lots of fruits and vegetables."

"Ha, ha," he said, oozing with charm. "What does running the booth entail?"

"Well, I'll spend Wednesday and Thursday gathering, baking, and packaging. Friday, I'll set up the produce and products I hope to sell…maybe decorate my booth a little, if I have enough time. The festival starts that afternoon. The vendor hall opens that evening."

"How long does the festival last?"

"Through Sunday; although, I hope I've sold everything by Saturday night so I can spend Sunday afternoon taking it all down."

"Do you have someone to help with the weekend?"

"Not really."

"You can't do all that by yourself," Teddy protested.

"I *can*. I have before, and I will many times again," Baylin corrected. "But I won't have to; whoever's around will be more than happy to lend a hand here and there throughout the festival."

"Huh," Teddy grunted.

Baylin cast up a quick prayer of thanksgiving that he'd run out of conversational steam.

4

"Here," Baylin said, handing Teddy a sticky note. He read the name and number she'd written on it.

"What's this?"

"A talented mechanic."

His stomach soured.

"I don't know," he said, his words laden with apprehension.

"He's a wizard with engines."

Teddy hesitated, looking wearily at the slip of paper in his hand.

"I still don't know," he hedged. "Boxy isn't any ol' car."

"Jax isn't *any ol'* mechanic," she countered. "And you named your car?" The grimace on her face spoke volumes.

"Uh, yeah!" Didn't everyone?

"Boxy? Is that a play on Foxy? Or Roxy?"

Teddy wanted to kiss that scrunched up snooty expression

right off her beautiful face. Wait— *Wipe* that look away, not kiss. What was he thinking?

"Nooo," Teddy replied, shaking off the strange and displaced urge. "She's a—"

"*She?*"

"Of course."

"Wow," she stated. Her eyes brightened, and Teddy would have sworn she fought back a giggle.

"Please, do continue with this riveting tale," she said, bowing forward as if extending an invitation.

"*She*," Teddy emphasized, "is a vintage racing car. In racing, when cars go back to their garage — their home, so to speak, for the event — they're told to *box*. And, as a kid playing baseball, I always felt at home in the batter's box. So, I named her Boxy."

A speechless Baylin meant she was dumbfounded by his idiocy or impressed by his cleverness. Teddy feared knowing which one she felt at that moment.

"Well, call Jax. That's his cell; he'll answer, even on a Sunday night. *Boxy* will be safe in his hands. I promise," she tacked on with a saucy head shake.

When Baylin left the kitchen, Teddy pulled out a chair and sat down to make the dreaded call.

Not thirty seconds later, she returned with a laptop computer.

She set it in front of him and pointed to the screen.

"These are your lodging options. Start calling them after you talk to Jax," she ordered. Then she walked to the back door, slid on a highlighter orange beanie, and put on a heavy plaid flannel jacket.

"Where are you going?" he called just as she closed the door on her way out.

She ignored him.

Teddy was on the phone when she walked back through

the kitchen thirty minutes later, replaced her winter gear, and disappeared down the hallway without a second glance in his direction.

Another twenty-five minutes later, feeling much worse about his hotel options but much better about his car, Teddy slid his chair back under the table, switched off the kitchen lights, and wandered down the hall in search of Baylin.

Before he found her, Teddy discovered an old-fashioned parlor that encompassed the double-door entryway and stretched the width of the house, which he guessed was built in in the very early 1900s. His slight obsession with historical architecture and house design forced his feet into the room.

He envisioned the space as it likely had been a century before: an elegant center of the home, perfect for entertaining, with formal furniture, grand artwork and sculptures, patterned wallpaper, and tons of natural light streaming through the oversized picture windows. Teddy imagined men sitting in tall-backed chairs while smoking and discussing business…solving the problems of the world. He pictured women in full skirts and upswept hair, chatting about families in their community and *actually* solving the problems of *their* world. The room carried an air of timeless stability.

He brushed off the creative history he'd conjured and studied the room for real.

Over the years, updates had transformed the parlor into a less formal room, one spacious enough to serve multiple purposes. Half the space felt solid and masculine, stately but not stuffy. Ornate carvings decorated rich wooden end tables and matched a heavy coffee table. Upholstered wingback chairs, a leather sofa, and an antique upright piano added layers of colors and textures. The layout resembled a private library.

Indeed, it *was* a private library. Floor-to-ceiling built-in bookshelves dominated the entire side wall on that end of the room. Handsome, four-sided bookcases dotted the open space. Books, artwork, knick-knacks, and portraits in all ages and fashions of frames filled every shelf to the gills.

Outside of school and city libraries, Teddy had never seen such a wonderful collection of books. Some spines appeared older than dirt, but much richer with metallic lettering and embossed designs on the weathered leather covers. Others looked to be straight out of the late 1900s with glossy dust jackets printed in bold, vivid colors to show off bubbly, artistic fonts and dramatic scenes hinting at the stories tucked inside.

One large section of shelving contained a collection of books in individual cardboard slipcases. Their pristine condition belied their obvious age. Teddy picked up an edition of *Adventures of Huckleberry Finn,* one of his all-time favorites, and eased the book from its case. With gentle caution, he opened the cover, but just a little so as not to pull on the spine. Inside lay a brochure, a single page folded in half to create four pages of detailed information. He read the contents cover to cover, learning about the typesetting and illustrator and binding used for that edition.

Teddy replaced the Mark Twain novel to explore *Candide* by Voltaire. The same type of brochure, with the title *Sandglass* under the words *The Heritage Club,* rested inside the cover again. He found one in every book he glanced in. He admired a beautiful copy of *Through the Looking-Glass,* Lewis Carroll's sequel to *Alice in Wonderland.* A lovely bouquet, stamped in white foil, filled the cornflower blue cover, equally simple and elegant. Then Teddy stumbled upon an exquisite copy of *The Pickwick Papers* by Charles Dickens. A rope pattern framed the letters *CD,* all of which were embossed with deep red ink that matched the slipcase. A shiny gold foil circle displayed the title on the binding. Hands down, it was the most fabulous book Teddy had ever seen.

He held a strong affinity for Dickens; he related to Dickensian characters deep in his soul.

Without conscious thought, Teddy settled into an overstuffed reading chair positioned close to the bookshelves. He pulled the chain on a floor lamp over his left shoulder. As though he'd received a delicate treasure, Teddy studied the title page, *The Posthumous Papers of the Pickwick Club*. A wonderful drawing with the caption, *Mr. Snodgrass The Poet*, faced the title page. The vivid colors brought the character, in all his conflicted romantic melancholy, to life. The man's personality oozed from the artwork.

Teddy turned the page to find the copyright information: a first edition printed in 1938, by The Heritage Press, Inc., illustrated by Gordon Ross. *Magnificent*.

With the greatest of care, Teddy laid open the Sandglass — *Number XII: 26* — and began reading about the birth of Samuel Pickwick. *Fascinating*.

"They won't break," Baylin announced from the doorframe, where she leaned against one shoulder, indicating she'd been there a minute.

Busted.

"They might," Teddy argued. "They're extraordinary."

"That they are," she agreed. *She agreed*…with something Teddy said. *Miracles never cease*.

"And my family has a fantastic collection of them," Baylin explained.

"How many are there?"

"A man named George Macy published them as a monthly book club from 1935 to 1982, with a few bonus releases from time to time; they only ran about fifteen thousand copies per printing, just enough for their subscribers. So, roughly fifty years…that's about six hundred titles…times fifteen thousand copies—"

"Nine million books," Teddy finished for her. "In the publishing world, that's not many."

"Unless you're an author trying to sell them, in which case nine million books is a decent number," Baylin contested.

"*Touché*," he allowed, enjoying their back-and-forth banter. She wanted to stay aloof, to shut him out. But, she wasn't fooling Teddy. She liked him, at least a little.

"Why do you smile so much? Or grin? Or just…be happy?"

"Would you prefer I be grumpy and cross?"

"Maybe," she said, crossing to the bookcase to pick up two Heritage Press Club books, both matching with emerald green binding and canary yellow slipcases. Teddy couldn't read the gold foil imprinted titles from across the room.

Baylin perched on a second reading chair close to where Teddy sat, handing the top book to him before sliding the book in her lap from its case.

"*Gone with the Wind*, Margaret Mitchell, Number 1," he read aloud.

"Hmm," she hummed. "These are my favorite in the collection." Teddy followed her lead as he'd done in the garden, opening the volume and flipping until he came to an elaborate double-page illustration, a sketched and colored scene straight from the height of antebellum finery. He glanced to see Baylin's illustration depicted a post-battle scene of the Civil War. Where the artwork in his volume promised youth and hope and possibility, the artwork in her volume portrayed bleakness, pain, and death.

Teddy watched Baylin run her fingers over the pages. Then she exhaled, as though shaking off sadness. She closed the book and went to replace it. Teddy did the same. He stopped to stand just behind her shoulder, reaching over and around to return his volume.

Was it rude to invade her space? Nah, he just wanted to see how she'd respond.

Too bad that yet again, he didn't know if her reaction was a positive or a negative, if the way she stood her ground meant she didn't feel the air sizzling between them, or if she felt it but had the strength to hide it.

If so, she was stronger than Teddy.

His fingers itched to touch her hair, to move it aside and trace her jawline. Oh, to place his lips on the soft skin at the curve of her neck.

Man, had Cupid's arrow hit its mark, right dead center in the middle of Teddy's chest.

Reining in his wayward thoughts and even more outrageous desires for a woman he'd known less than twelve hours, one who didn't seem to feel the same…*yet*, Teddy stepped past Baylin to return the Dickens book to its empty slot on the shelf. He might've let his body brush hers as he went by. Just a hint of touch.

He wasn't a saint, after all.

5

Old MacDonald Had a Farm
Traditional children's nursery rhyme ~
Thought to have been written by
Thomas d'Urfey for an opera in 1706

"Y ou were right about Jax Fielding. I just got off the phone with him, and the man knows cars, even vintage German roadsters," Teddy announced.

"Just as I suspected," she said with her most charming know-it-all smirk.

Baylin crossed the wide expanse of the parlor, the part that felt like the most inviting living room in the world…her favorite spot on earth, next to her sewing studio upstairs and the horse stalls in the barn and the garden plots.

Maybe I like this entire place a little too much?

She bent to adjust the logs on the fireplace grate, lit a match, and turned the key to light the gas starter. Satisfied with the fire, she closed the screen and picked up a project from the game table, which stood in the room's corner. Then Baylin plopped down on the deep-seated, rolled-arm, overstuffed sofa, quilt in hand, to begin hand-stitching the binding around the edges. She needed to finish before Wednesday, when she'd submit her Valentine's quilt for judging in the weekend's competition.

The work in progress merged her love of crisp, clean backgrounds and the festival's theme: Conversation Hearts. Baylin had pieced heart-shaped blocks in boisterous reds, pretty pinks, and warm peaches; the random prints created a scrappy vibe, while their precise placement on an oyster-white solid broadcloth established structure and stability. She'd machine-quilted custom motifs in unique patterns…a time-consuming process, but one that produced a one-of-a-kind quilt. Baylin had named the design *Speaking of Love* because it reminded her of candy hearts, a handful of sweet nothings that provide joy and delight. The Busy Bees' Quilt Guild consisted of unbelievably talented quilters and fiber artists, so Baylin didn't expect to win the contest, but sharing it with the world brought its own reward.

Teddy scanned the other bookshelves as he weaved through the parlor. He meandered with patience, making his way to the wide recliner beside her big comfy couch.

"This is quite a chair," he acknowledged, flipping the handle to extend the footrest. "Easily large enough for two."

She ignored his teasing reference.

"That also looks like quite a quilt."

The admiration in his tone caused a strange response in her nerves. A flush of pride heated her cheeks. She admonished the reaction; his praise meant nothing…less than nothing, really.

But even as she thought the thought, she stood in front of him, shaking the quilt to hang flat from her grasp so he could see the full design.

Baylin's pulse quickened. She had put an enormous amount of time into designing the block layout, playing with how she wanted to piece the heart shapes, writing the steps to follow to make it, illustrating the instructions, and pulling a variety of fabrics in eclectic prints and compatible colors, not to mention the hours it took to cut the pieces, sew them back together, load the longarm machine, and quilt the layers together. Without a word or even a sound — odd for Theodore Gwenn, it seemed — he lowered the recliner and stood to study the quilt. Teddy leaned close to the fabric and looked over every heart-shaped block. He grinned, nodding his approval when he noticed a scrap of a vintage-styled baseball print in reds and pinks, and locked eyes with her.

Her breath caught. She wanted Teddy to realize it was much more than a pile of fabric; Baylin needed him to see that she'd put part of herself into the creation.

"It's a work of art," he said, not joking, and not laughing… but with sincere deference.

"I hope the judges agree," she said, her voice softer than she'd intended. "It's the first quilt I've entered in a competition. I'm not sure how it'll stack up to the others, but I figured it was worth a try. I mean—" Baylin cut off her rambling. "I hope they like it."

"They'd be blind not to," Teddy said, picking up the bottom edge and helping Baylin fold it back onto her lap as she sat down to continue sewing.

He returned to his seat on the recliner but kept both feet on the ground, leaning forward, resting his elbows on his knees while he watched her movements. His attention heightened Baylin's senses, and yet, she wouldn't have described the sensation as repulsive. If forced, she might've even admitted that his company was rather nice.

"What did Jax have to say?" Baylin asked, eager to move the conversation to topics *not* centered on herself, her quilting skills, or the project she'd prayed over for several weeks.

"I should've called him earlier in the day. He's going to

send a tow truck in the morning, but he won't be able to look at Boxy until Wednesday, maybe even Thursday. By the time he orders parts and waits for them to arrive, he suspects it'll be the middle of next week before I'm out of here."

When she didn't comment, Teddy continued.

"He also said I'd be hard-pressed to find a place to stay, that rooms in town are full for the festival. He thought me calling around to look for one would be a waste of time."

"Did he now?"

Baylin didn't look away from her stitching, didn't dare glance at his pleading puppy-dog eyes. Her peripheral vision betrayed her, though.

He scratched his head, as though working up the courage to ask the question she did *not* want him asking. He didn't even try to hide the guilty grin on his face.

"Couldn't I just stay here? With you?"

"Nope," Baylin answered, setting her quilt bundle to the side and standing to walk away. That's what Papa Joe had always advised: *If a situation takes a turn down a dangerous road, remove yourself from the situation.*

"Come on, Baylin. Please?" He followed her down the hall and up the stairs but halted when she entered her bedroom. "You won't even know I'm here."

"Fat chance of that," Baylin called over her shoulder as she stepped into her closet to retrieve a pair of house shoes she could wear in the truck.

He'd grated on her nerves with his incessant happiness, ceaseless chattering, and cheerful humming all afternoon. Even while washing dishes and scraping the skillet, he'd taken the concept of *whistle while you work* to an extra dimension. No way — *no how* — she would be unaware of his presence.

"Where am I supposed to go?" That fine line between charming and annoying might've worked for Teddy in the past, but not anymore...*not with Baylin O'Casey,* she vowed.

"Since Jax says there aren't any rooms in town, and you decided not to call and find out for yourself, I'll give you a ride to the Lodge." Problem solved.

"Where is that?"

"At Daisy Lake."

"How far away is Daisy Lake?"

"Eight miles back to Green Hills…fifteen miles to the lake."

"How am I supposed to get back to town in the morning?"

"Looks like you have two legs that work just fine," she pointed out with an indulgent smile.

"Thanks for noticing," he said, all jovial pride. "But seriously, what will I do out there for a week while Jax has Boxy?"

"Not my problem," she said with a shrug, suppressing the grin threatening to defeat her. Sparring with Teddy was fun. But not enough fun to relent! Or perhaps it would prove too much fun. That was Baylin's bigger fear. "Let's go," she ordered, leaving him to follow.

By the time Teddy reached the garage, Baylin had snapped her seatbelt into place and turned the key in the ignition, thankful the starter caught and the old truck engine came to life on her first attempt.

"Are you really going to abandon me at the lake?" he asked, again teetering between adorable and infuriating.

"You won't be the only one there." Baylin put the truck in reverse and eased out of the garage.

"Maybe not, but I'll probably be the only one *stranded* there."

"In which case," she pointed out, "plenty of people will be happy to take you wherever you want to go."

"I want to go here."

"Here is not an option for you."

"Why not?"

"Because *I* live here."

"Exactly," he agreed, causing another flutter in her chest, one she chose to ignore.

"What if there aren't any rooms left at the lodge?"

"Then they'll find an empty cabin that an owner rents short-term."

"What if there are no available cabins?"

"Then they have tents to rent for pitching on the campground."

"You have an answer for everything, don't you?" he asked in a backhanded-compliment kind of way. Teddy had tried to sound galled, but the ever-present smile in his eyes gave away his good humor.

"Yes," Baylin agreed. "Yes, I do."

He shook his head from side to side with an indulgent laugh, but he didn't comment.

She won. Theodore Gwenn had run out of questions, complaints, and requests.

They rode in peace and quiet as Baylin drove past the O'Casey Farm sign, turned onto the farm-to-market road bordering her land, and headed toward Teddy's car so he could retrieve his bags and belongings.

She'd claimed victory too soon; his silence lasted only until she'd pulled up behind his vehicle…*Boxy*.

"How much are they going to charge?"

"I guess that depends on which accommodation you have to settle for," she answered.

"What if I can't afford it?"

Teddy had turned to face Baylin in the cab of her beat-up old truck. Baylin faced the windshield, which provided a perfect view of the sleek red race car, illuminated by the head-lights she'd left on high beam.

Even at night, the fancy two-seater screamed *I'm a rare trea-sure!* Baylin's eyes skimmed the back fender, the bumper, the exposed seats. She couldn't find a smudge, much less a blemish.

"I'm going to go out on a limb and say you can find the funds if you try hard enough." She pinned him with a direct look, lifting a sarcastic eyebrow for effect.

"You might be right," he conceded with a slight bow of his head. "I *can* pay. In fact, I'm willing to pay… I'm willing to pay to stay *here.*"

For the first time since their mock argument began, Teddy had Baylin's full, undivided attention. And the scoundrel knew it. She could tell.

In a split second, the gleam in his eyes brightened, and he doubled down his efforts to charm and convince her to join his side, to sweet-talk Baylin until she agreed with his way of thinking.

"It's going to be a few days before Boxy is road ready. That many nights will add up in rental fees. I'd sure rather those fees go to O'Casey Farm than anywhere else. I'll get my bags from the car; it'll take me a minute to put her cover on for the night. Be right back." Teddy tossed a quick wink in her direction before exiting the truck.

She watched him move in the spotlight of her truck. He took a backpack and a duffel bag from the car, lucky her's was the road less traveled and his possessions were sitting in his passenger seat after half the afternoon, all evening, and a few hours in the dark of night. After setting the bags on the road between their vehicles, he pulled a folded tan canvas from behind the seats, unfolded it with meticulous accuracy, and secured an industrial-sized elastic strap below the base of the car's body. Then he pocketed the keys, picked up his stuff, and returned to the truck. He set both his bags in the bed and climbed into his seat.

"Does that cover have a locking mechanism?"

"Yeah, it has a cable system sewn into the edge of the cover. It's supposed to be theft-proof, although I've never tried cutting through it, so that might be a marketing ploy."

"Couldn't someone just cut through the fabric? It looks like canvas."

"I'm sure if there's a will, there's a way, but again, it's seven layers of polypropylene and billed as the best available."

"Will Jax be able to tow it with the cover on?"

"Yeah, and it'll help protect Boxy while she's on the tow truck." Somehow, the way he called the car by name had stopped sounding ridiculous and started sounding cute.

Lord, help me.

Baylin put the truck in gear. Teddy snapped his seatbelt.

But she didn't take her foot off the brake.

"$100 a night," she spat.

"Okay," he agreed.

"Fine. $200 a night," she said, doubling her original offer.

"Done."

"$400 a night," she amended, challenging him. Hoping he'd say *no?*

Or praying he'd say *yes?*

"You drive a hard bargain," he said with a sly smile. "But I'm good for it."

"$500 a night," she declared, throwing down the gauntlet. "That's my final offer."

"$500 a night," he repeated, still wearing that victorious smile like a badge of honor. "It's a deal."

"Five hundred dollars a night," she repeated, just to hear the words one more time. "And you sleep in the barn."

It's nice to have a crush on someone.
It feels like you're alive, you know?
Scarlett Johansson

"With the animals?"

Baylin didn't answer until after she'd made a U-turn and headed back in the direction of the farm, her house, and his apparent barn.

"With the pigs and the horses and the chickens?" He tried again, for clarity of the situation and such.

"You'll survive."

"In the winter?"

"We're in southeast Oklahoma," she reminded him.

"Where it's rather chilly," he pointed out.

"I promise you'll be just fine," Baylin said, teasing or cajoling. Teddy couldn't be sure which.

"And what about mice? Or snakes?" he asked.

"We have barn cats to take care of the mice, and it's too cold out for snakes this time of year. Nothing to worry about," she said, flashing a happy, reassuring smile his way. The fact

Baylin was happy all of a sudden, maybe even *gleeful,* did the opposite of reassuring Teddy.

He held his tongue for the rest of the drive.

In reality, sleeping on the ground, under the stars, with all God's creatures, wouldn't have worried Teddy. He'd grown up in Watson, Louisiana, a small town not unlike Green Hills, Oklahoma, where boys hunted and fished and ran around the countryside with their brothers and buddies every chance they could.

The only difference between where he'd come from and where he stood in that moment? Alligators…there weren't any alligators to wrestle in southeast Oklahoma.

Were there?

"Baylin?"

"Yeah?"

They'd arrived and parked the truck in the garage. He'd grabbed his bags and moved to follow her into the house.

She stopped on the stoop, blocking his path, and turned an innocent, yet inquisitive eye his way.

"Are there alligators in Oklahoma?"

"Sure, in some rivers and streams, but they tend to stay south and east of here."

"Great," Teddy muttered under his breath.

"Barn's that way," she said with a little head tilt toward the massive, rather hard to miss, red building about thirty yards from the house. "Goodnight."

Baylin went inside and closed the door.

He heard the deadbolt lock click into place.

And then she turned out the lights. All the lights.

Is a sassy red-headed vixen more dangerous than a cold-blooded reptile?

He chuckled at the thought.

No tour of the barn, no *I'll see you tomorrow,* no anything at all.

Standing on the stoop of her side entrance in the pitch dark of night, Teddy tried to remember the last time he'd felt such an encouraging wave of anticipation.

As he trudged to the tall red barn, a smile planted itself on his face.

Baylin O'Casey was just his type of challenge, the kind of puzzle he liked to solve.

Thinking back on their encounters throughout the day, his smile grew to a full-fledged grin.

However long it took to see Boxy repaired promised to be an interesting, unpredictable adventure.

The barn turned out to be the first curveball…

Teddy rolled back one of the heavy doors to reveal a first-rate barndominium.

A gigantic green tractor monopolized the center of the building, with a couple of smaller tractors and two ATVs parked down the left side. An office, an equipment and supply room, and open tack storage lined the right side.

Teddy followed the sound of gentle nickers and neighs to discover three horse stalls and a series of working pens, each with doors opening to the pasture behind the barn.

"Your owner is something else," Teddy told the first horse, the chestnut mare Baylin had been riding that morning. Feisty — like her master — the ginger-coated beauty gave an annoyed sigh as Teddy moved to her side so she could see him better. When she'd settled, he lifted a gentle hand to pet her neck and shoulder. The iron nameplate on the front of her stall introduced her as Penelope. "Are you a loyal and faithful steed?" he asked the horse. "I bet so," Teddy cooed to the beast. "I bet Baylin instills that in everyone she meets, man and farm animal alike. She really is *something else*."

He spent a moment with the other two horses, named Phoebe and Eros. Then he made his way up the circular, wrought-iron stairs leading to a second story over the office and storerooms, where windows overlooking the open expanse of the barn glowed with soft yellow light.

Someone had left a light on for him.

The condo portion of the barn rivaled any dorm or apartment Teddy'd inhabited during his journey through college and the minors.

The door at the top of the stairs opened to a cozy living area. A soft and inviting brown leather sectional the color of tobacco filled most of the room. Quilts in a variety of sizes and colors covered the rungs of a rustic wooden ladder. An armchair upholstered in a southwestern print paid homage to Native American artistry. A television hung over a gas log fireplace that *someone* had left burning to warm the space. Between the rock fireplace facing and the large sofa, a square coffee table held an assortment of decorative and necessary items such as the television remote, a stack of *Western Art Collector* magazines, a set of sandstone coasters, two large-format photography books, playing cards in a box, a square box of tissues, a leather-scented candle, and a binder with instructions for the TV, fireplace, thermostat, and Wi-Fi.

After rifling through the *accoutrements*, Teddy glanced around the kitchen. The stocked cabinets contained a plethora of pots, pans, and cookie sheets. In the fridge he found a glass pitcher of milk, a bowl of fresh fruit, a few single-serve yogurts, and two jars of homemade jam. A box of dry cereal, a bag of granola, and three blueberry muffins — each covered in plastic wrap and tied with a ribbon — filled a basket on the countertop. A coffee pot and a pouch of fresh ground beans sat beside the basket. Plates, cups, mugs, bowls, silverware, and fringe-trimmed cloth napkins provided an eye-catching and useful setting on the small round table. Each of the four dining chairs held a pillow made from a quilt block; the pillow trim matched the napkins. *Someone* had put an awful lot of work into creating stylish yet functional guest quarters.

Designed like the shotgun houses he knew from Louisiana, the condo's layout led from living space to kitchen to utility room to bedroom to bathroom. At about eighteen feet wide, it used every inch of space, yet nothing felt cramped. And in every room, the same intentional care had gone into selecting comfortable furniture, attractive finishes, and all the amenities a guest could need.

Someone did an outstanding job putting it together.

After a quick shower, Teddy climbed into bed in the way-more-than-adequate lodgings. He inhaled the sharp, woodsy scent of the crisp, fresh-laundered linens.

And he thought of that *someone*.

7

Think in the morning.
Act in the noon.
Eat in the evening.
Sleep in the night.
William Blake

After sending Teddy to the barn, Baylin took a quick shower and returned to the parlor. By the light of her laptop, she surveyed the items remaining on the day's checklist. Baylin checked and answered emails, reconciled the farm accounts and paid bills, printed packing slips for orders from the farm's online store, noted which items to restock, and reviewed Monday's to-do list. With those chores done, she checked doors, adjusted the thermostat, and headed to her room. At 11 o'clock sharp, Baylin turned back the covers and quilts on her bed, climbed in, and closed her eyes.

But sleep evaded her.

Instead of the dark oblivion she typically enjoyed after a long Sunday of early morning chores followed by church and lunch in town, an afternoon of making up for the morning off, and an evening of preparing for the week ahead, Teddy appeared in her mind.

He was easy on the eyes, no denying that.

At five foot seven, Baylin didn't consider herself short, but also not tall. Teddy towered over her; he had to be at least six foot two. But not lanky. No, he filled out his faded blue jeans and soft cotton t-shirt quite nicely.

His well-worn boots, muscular build, natural tan, and *aw-shucks* approach to life led her to believe he worked with his hands, not behind a desk where he'd wear a suit and tie and sit in a quiet cubicle day after day. Baylin understood people who worked outdoors, doing physical labor... Those were her people.

Once upon a time, Baylin had considered a sophisticated, fancy-dressing corporate type life in a city. She'd applied to colleges all over the country and accepted a scholarship to attend the business school at Southern Methodist University. Dallas wasn't too far of a drive from Green Hills and living in Big D had sounded glitzy and glamorous. SMU's campus and the buzz of energy she felt when she visited for her admissions interview sold her on the adventure. She'd even dreamed of staying there for law school after earning her undergraduate degree. Excited for the future and eager for the unknown, Baylin had been open to wherever the path led.

But a week before her high school graduation, tragedy struck.

Papa Joe died in a freak farming accident. One minute he'd been strong and healthy; the next minute he'd been gone.

Grandma, who'd been showing early signs of dementia, couldn't handle the farm by herself, wouldn't have known what farm work to do daily even without the memory challenges. The house and garden had always been her domain, the crops and animals had been Papa Joe's.

And Baylin's.

Since she'd been big enough to sit on a pony and carry a feed bucket, Baylin had been Papa Joe's constant companion on the farm. She'd lived in town with her parents, but she'd spent every available second, every weekend, and every school break on the O'Casey Farm.

After Papa Joe's sudden death, Baylin canceled her plan to attend SMU so she could help her family. When her parents announced plans to sell the farm and find an assisted living community for Grandma, Baylin gave up on going away *to* college. Instead, she completed her studies online and at a different school, one known for the new degree she sought: agricultural business and farm management.

The business degree had come in handy since she'd bought out her parents' financial interest in the farm. In the five and a half years she'd been running it, they'd expanded the operation. She'd worked alongside the Sharp family, who owned the most successful ranching enterprise in the area, if not the entire state of Oklahoma. Hudson Sharp and his aunt Juniper had advised and mentored Baylin. They'd been a surrogate family since her mom and dad moved to Florida. Between her dad's inheritance and the funds they received from selling to Baylin, her parents had the means to retire from her dad's job as a local insurance agent and her mom's job as the elementary school secretary.

Besides the icky feeling that Papa Joe's death had made it possible, Baylin had no qualms with her parents' decision to leave. The farm had never been their thing, and they'd only stayed in Green Hills so long for Baylin to grow up there, in a safe community and surrounded by friends and loved ones. They loved their life in Florida, and Baylin loved that for them.

Meanwhile, Baylin's life revolved around the O'Casey farm.

She oversaw every aspect, worked *in* the business, not just on it. Her hands got dirty every single day. That's why she understood a farmer's tan, thread-bare blue jeans, and scuffed boots.

On the other hand, those boots had cost a pretty penny; Baylin could tell that by the quality of the leather and the stitching on them.

And that car! *Boxy*.

Somewhere amidst Teddy's constant stream of chatter and singing and humming and chuckling, it became obvious that Teddy was very well-spoken…like someone not only educated but trained in public speaking.

On top of that, Teddy seemed drawn to her library; he'd been so reverent with each book he touched. Working long days outdoors left little time to read; Baylin could attest to that… Her *to be read* list rivaled Santa's book of names.

Those thoughts of books she wanted to read and the Dickens novel Teddy'd chosen, of the piano piece she needed to perfect for the festival's pageant and the way Teddy seemed to have an endless song on his lips, of the bubble bath she eschewed for a quick shower to save time because she'd spent too much time with Teddy that night, of the way his jeans moved with his easy gait, of the way he hustled to carry the potato crates so she wouldn't have to heft the heavy load, of the way Teddy—

Grrrr! Teddy, Teddy, Teddy.

He'd consumed her thoughts all night, when she should've been sleeping.

When the alarm chimed bright and early at 5:30 a.m., Baylin didn't greet the day with a smile.

When Teddy knocked on the side door entrance to the kitchen at 7:00 a.m., Baylin still wasn't smiling.

But Teddy was.

His glass-half-full, permanent-good-mood aura accomplished the dual effects of irritating Baylin while lifting her spirits at the same time.

Grrrr, again.

"Good morning," he offered, taking his grin up a notch. "Mind if I share a cup of coffee with you?"

"Help yourself; burner's still on." Baylin gestured toward the pot.

"Can I pour a mug for you?"

"No, I don't have time," she answered. Despite her protest, he poured two cups.

She frowned when he set them both on the table and pulled out a chair for her.

"I don't—" she began, but he cut her off.

"I heard you," he admitted. They both knew good and well he'd heard her. "But the day's gonna fly by quick enough; we might as well take a few minutes to enjoy it before it's gone."

"Humph," she grunted indelicately, prompting him to giggle.

Giggle!

Did adult men giggle? Ever?

Someone should outlaw giggling first thing in the morning!

Resigned to drink the cup of coffee he'd made for her — just so it wouldn't go to waste — Baylin grabbed the creamer from the refrigerator and joined Teddy at the table.

She ignored him as she added sugar and cream and stirred her drink, aware he watched her every move.

She lifted the cup to inhale the aroma, closed her eyes, and sipped the hot brew. Baylin couldn't stop the satisfied sigh that escaped after her first taste.

Like clockwork, Baylin made a pot of coffee every morning, just in case she'd hired farm hands for the day and one stopped by with questions. Baylin rarely poured herself a cup. And she never sat down to drink it. Doing so used up precious minutes she needed to tackle other tasks.

She'd been missing out.

Teddy had the wisdom not to say *I told you so*, but his gleeful smile said it for him.

"Did you eat?" she asked.

"Yes, thank you. *Someone* left yogurt and fruit and these amazing muffins. They were delicious."

"And the barn is adequate for your stay?"

"More than," he confirmed. "Again, someone set it up just right."

He paused, and Baylin nodded, feeling obligated to acknowledge his compliment but adamantly refusing to let him know she was the one who'd made the muffins the day before, she'd decorated the barndominium when they added it to the barn a few years earlier, and she'd taken a few minutes to get it ready for Teddy while he'd called Jax about his car.

He's nothing but grief.

By the end of their afternoon in the garden the previous day, Baylin had considered letting him rent the condo. Then she'd reprimanded herself for even thinking such a thing. But then she'd softened during dinner and run upstairs to be sure he had some food and necessities to make his stay enjoyable. She'd wanted the space to be warm and inviting for him, just in case he didn't find a hotel room. The moment that thought ran through her head, she had promptly scolded herself for being weak and had mentally put her foot down: *Teddy Gwenn needs to go.*

That he hadn't even tried to find a hotel room proved it!

But she'd caved a third time when she'd been sitting in her truck as he gathered his bags. Watching him talk to his ridiculous car while he handled it with kid gloves tugged at her heartstrings.

All that wishy-washy emotional stuff gave Baylin a headache. She'd take the fact that Teddy consumed so much — or *any* — of her thoughts to the grave. There was no telling what he'd have done with the information.

"Want me to pay you each morning?" He reached for his back pocket. "$500 per day, I believe." She smirked at the teasing twinkle in his eyes.

"One check at the end will be fine." Baylin pushed back from the table and stood, slid in her chair, and stepped to the sink. She finished her coffee, savoring the last drop. She rinsed the mug and set it in the dishwasher. Then she walked to the coat rack by the door, selected a sherpa-lined work jacket, and opened the door. Just before she headed to the chicken coop to collect eggs, she glanced back over her shoulder to meet Teddy's gaze. "And yes, $500 per day will suffice," she added with a little shoulder shake of snootiness.

By golly, two can play that game!

8

**If you've broken the eggs,
you should make the omelette.
Anthony Eden**

Teddy didn't waste any time, quickly rinsing his mug and setting it in the dishwasher. He glanced around the kitchen…spic-and-span, just as he would've guessed.

Before he flew out the door in Baylin's wake, Teddy noticed a spiral notebook on the countertop. She'd left it open to an extensive list of tasks:

Finish quilt (take photos!)
Deliver quilt to Miss Sadie
Merch for booth:
- FQ bundles (press and tie)
- Napkins
- Tablecloths
- Pillows

- Soaps (finish packaging)
- Farm tees
- Valentine's apparel
- Vintage boxes
- Postcards
- Sticker display
- Bookmarks
- Food and produce for booth:
- Butter
- Eggs
- Goat cheese
- Jams and jellies
- Salsa
- Canned fruits
- Peaches
- Pears
- Apple pie filling
- Blackberry pie filling
- Cherry pie filling
- Black-eyed peas
- Green beans

The list went on and on for pages.

No one person could get this much done. *Good grief, when does she sleep?*

Teddy flipped off the coffeemaker, turned off the lights, and dashed to find his hostess.

Because she needed some help.

He spotted her in a fenced yard, clucking to chickens while tossing feed in the same manner the brusque February wind tossed the long waves of her red hair. No, not red…and less auburn than it had looked indoors. The bright early morning sun turned it copper in color.

Trade her form-fitting, curve-defining modern blue jeans for a long skirt, and in that setting, she could've traveled to anytime in history. She embodied the image of a strong, hard-working woman greeting the day with chores on her farm… could've been pre-Civil War, the 1920s, or turn of the twenty-first century. She would be a ravishing beauty in any era.

On that day in 2021, the vision Baylin created across the yard did strange things to Teddy's equilibrium. And to his heart! He rubbed his chest to calm a flutter.

When she disappeared inside the chicken coop, Teddy shook off his daydream and jogged over to see how he could assist.

"Want some help?" he asked from the doorway, startling Baylin into dropping an egg.

"No," she replied with a smirk.

"Oops. Sorry," he said, chagrined. "Need me to clean that up?"

"No," she repeated, her voice short, flat, and final.

"I'm great at cleaning up messes."

"I can imagine."

"And I'm a terrific helper," Teddy added, stepping into the chicken coop and casting a glance around the space for a way to lend a hand. Besides roosting boxes, bars for perching, chickens, and wood shavings on the floor, the building was mostly empty. He didn't see a broom or rake or anything to work with. An air-tight container stood in one corner and a half-full, five-gallon water bucket sat upside-down in a metal base, which plugged into the wall.

"I could fill up this water dispens—"

"It's fine," Baylin interrupted. "I'm about done."

"Surely there's something I can do." Teddy turned a circle

in the relatively small space, shuffling to step around Baylin, but remaining in her way instead.

That earned him another admonishing look of exasperation.

"I'm finished feeding, and the water heater's set for the night. Hens don't lay as many eggs during the winter, so there are fewer to gather."

"At least let me carry some, so we don't drop more," he added, taking the egg basket from her without asking permission first.

"*We*, huh?"

Teddy confirmed with a slight nod and a playful wink.

"Do the heat lamps help?" he asked, gesturing to the box heaters glowing orange in each corner of the coop.

"They keep the chickens alive, and extra feed helps, but the chickens use most of their energy staying warm. That leaves little to spend on laying eggs." She reached under a hen to retrieve two more and handed them to Teddy. The basket remained less than a third full.

"Does this give you enough to sell at the festival? Minus the one I need to pay for, of course."

Baylin's posture relaxed a fraction at his self-effacing guilt. She took back her basket with a tug and set it on a wooden shelf.

"Yes, I've been collecting them for weeks. I have a bunch..." Baylin held her apron to create a bowl for the eggs and emptied the basket. "...even without that prized, golden egg on the ground," she said with a teasing smile.

Oh, I could get used to that smile.

Their eyes locked, right there in the middle of squawking and pecking and the smell of chickens. They both froze for a split second, just a ripple in time, but enough to create that sizzle in Teddy's chest again.

Glancing down, Baylin tucked a strand of hair behind her

ear. Then she looked into his eyes once more and stepped around him with a faint, "Excuse me."

"Oh here, I'll take some," Teddy offered.

She hesitated.

"They're safe. I promise," he pledged. "I'm good with my hands."

Her eyebrows shot up and her chin tilted.

"I mean, at using my hands," he said, tripping over the words while suppressing a laugh. "At catching things," he added. "Usually."

She continued to eye him with uncertainty, but he'd have sworn a little laughter bubbled behind her eyes.

"What I'm trying to say is that I won't drop any eggs." Teddy held out his hands for Baylin to fill with fresh eggs. She stacked them in his large palms until her apron was empty. "Where do they go?"

"Down the back hallway, there's a walk-in pantry next to the kitchen. You'll find a stack of empty cartons on the shelf by the green refrigerator. The eggs go in the cartons, and the cartons go in the fridge," she instructed.

"Do I need to wash them first?"

"No, they last longer if you don't."

He nodded and moved toward the house. Then he stopped mid-stride.

"Wanna go with me?"

"To the house?"

"Yeah."

"Why?"

"To put away the eggs," he answered.

"I thought you wanted to do that."

"I do," he was quick to reassure. "We could do it together."

"I don't know," she stalled. "I have a lot to do."

"Many hands make light work," he cajoled.

"So they say."

"Come on, I need you to open the door," he urged. "We'll finish the eggs, and then I'll help you with the next item on your list."

She looked him up and down, as though searching for a hidden agenda, but then she agreed, and they walked side by side toward the house.

Teddy fought the urge to juggle all the eggs into his left hand so he could entwine the fingers of his right hand with hers, mere inches away.

"Did you read my list?"

Teddy's eyes snapped to hers at the accusation in her voice, but the sparkle in her dark umber eyes revealed she'd been joking.

"It's quite a list," he confirmed.

"That it is," she said in an anxious tone. "That it is." She expelled a deep sigh as she pushed open the door.

Teddy followed Baylin across the kitchen and into the pantry.

Pantry didn't accurately define the space…make that *room*.

Literally, a storeroom, floor-to-ceiling shelves lined the walls. The only breaks in the shelving created built-in nooks for two refrigerators, one in 1970s avocado and one even older in a zesty poppy red, and two upright freezers. Both of those were stainless steel, shiny and new.

Stacked jars of canned foods weighed down the shelves along two walls. The jars' contents reflected every color of the rainbow and showed off jellies, jams, salsas, sauces, whole fruits, snapped veggies, and a bunch of items Teddy couldn't name but guessed would be delicious. *Farm to table* took on a whole new meaning.

Wooden crates, just like the ones they'd used to gather potatoes, covered another wall. Bars of soap, candles, and honey filled some to the brim. Others sat empty, awaiting their goods. Decorative signs tied with a ribbon designated that each crate held a unique item, scent, or formula. The oils and spices she used to make the various products created an intoxicating blend of citrus, floral, and woodsy smells.

The fourth and final wall held wicker baskets in a multitude of shapes and sizes. About half were empty. Textiles and notions filled the other half...pillows, folded linens, rolled fabric, bags of buttons, spools of thread. Teddy recognized them as hand-dyed goods only because his mother had done much of that work for their family when he was a kid and money was scarce.

Teddy stepped closer to the shelves, reading tags and admiring the plethora of goods.

"Curiouser and curiouser!" Teddy said, flashing a wide-eyed, knowing look in Baylin's direction and feeling another unexpected jolt of awareness when their eyes met.

She didn't respond, though, instead bustling about to snatch eggs, two at a time from the bowl of Teddy's hands, filling a carton, and depositing it in the green refrigerator.

Without another word, Baylin left him there. No doubt she'd scurried off to tackle another task.

Shaking his head, Teddy turned off the light and followed Baylin with an indulgent grin.

My little rabbit is on the run.

9

You can have everything in life you want,
if you will just help other people
get what they want.
Zig Ziglar

aylin fell into bed at her usual time, exhausted after a long day, but also restless with an energy that bubbled just beneath her skin.

With Teddy's help, she'd checked a decent number of items off her never-ending list of chores.

With Teddy's help…

Staring at her ceiling, images of Teddy helping throughout the day invaded her brain.

Teddy in the henhouse. Teddy feeding the goats. Teddy singing while making them sandwiches for lunch and whistling while cleaning up after they ate. Teddy saddling Eros without needing instructions, keeping up while they rode fence lines, checking for breaks, and murmuring to the horses while brushing their coats after their ride.

Teddy, Teddy, Teddy.

Again. *Ugh!*

Baylin flounced to her side, abusing her pillow with a few punches for good measure.

She hated to admit that having him around was nice.

Having someone to talk to throughout the day, to share the workload with, to laugh at when he was goofy — which was all the time — was also nice.

Maybe more than nice.

Baylin rolled to her stomach, burying her face in the mattress.

She didn't want to like him. She *really* didn't.

Guys like Teddy Gwenn — hunky, handsome, sweet, funny, book-loving, *hot* guys — didn't fall from the sky. They didn't quote *Alice in Wonderland,* get lost in Dickens, and whisper sweet nothings to her horses.

And they never stayed.

Not long-term.

No, whatever or whoever supplied Teddy with a rare, collectable, and very expensive car would expect something big from him in return, something *not* in Green Hills. The job that came with a schedule so flexible he could drop everything to spend a week helping on a farm in Oklahoma, would call him back to duty. He'd go back to his own life, and the sooner, the better.

Baylin had avoided asking him personal questions.

She didn't want to know his story, wasn't interested in his history...or what made him so stinkin' jolly all the blasted time...or why he'd been on Road 214, just beyond her slice of heaven, when his precious *Boxy* had broken down.

Baylin had no desire to meet his family or friends.

She didn't care what other books and authors he liked to read, didn't wonder why the sun had bleached light streaks in his thick, dark hair smack-dab in the middle of winter. She hadn't even noticed how his tall frame should've been wiry, but was deceptively strong instead.

Liar.

If she'd been legally blind, she still would have noticed the way his neck muscles corded and his shoulders filled out his flannel shirt while they'd been moving hay bales that afternoon.

Baylin rolled onto her back again, grabbed her pillow, and considered suffocating herself with it.

She gave up on sleep for the time being, slid on a thick robe and slippers, and crept downstairs to retrieve her spiral notebook. In the kitchen, the tea kettle caught her eye, and a cup of calming hot tea promised to soothe her frazzled nerves.

While the water heated, Baylin read through her to-do list, checking off tasks she and Teddy had completed and making notes of what else needed attention. She had developed her method of tracking chores and reminders back in high school, when juggling homework and group projects, volleyball practices and games, and extra-curricular activities like student government and FFA competitions filled her days to the point of overflowing.

Since then, she'd perfected the system to coordinate the farm's day-to-day operations, to track finances, and to keep up with her numerous side gigs and community obligations, which she loved doing. She'd also learned what it *actually* meant to be pulled in so many directions she'd never, ever catch up.

Baylin had become a top-rate logistics expert, putting out fires wherever they popped up, and she prided herself on extinguishing them at a very high level.

She jotted down a few last-minute ideas for her booth at the Sweetheart Festival. From sunup to sundown, Teddy had refused to give her a moment's peace. If he remained that determined to shadow her every step, she might as well put him to good use, which meant some of the merchandise she'd taken off the inventory list could go back on. With his help, she'd be able to tag, price, and package more of the textile products…perhaps even more of the goat milk soaps that had been great sellers the year before.

Deep in thought and crunching the numbers, Baylin jumped out of her chair when the kettle whistled. After fixing her tea, she returned to her spiral notebook, her pages of plans…her happy place. Running the farm challenged her in the best ways, pushing her creativity while tapping into her need to make things neat and tidy.

By the time she'd finished her tea, she'd filled in another sheet of bullet points. The lavender and chamomile brew had done its job, and her eyelids drooped.

As Baylin rinsed her teacup, she might've glanced out the window and across the yard toward the barn, out of habit. She wasn't looking for lights, and she *wasn't* looking for a man.

Even one who meandered back into her thoughts as she climbed into bed and drifted off to sleep.

*T*uesday morning, Baylin couldn't remember her dreams, but judging by her pervading sense of peace and restfulness, she suspected they'd been nice.

Just as the sun peeked over the horizon, she skipped down the stairs with a pleasant excitement thrumming through her veins. Community events, in particular the Christmas and Valentine's Day festivals, put a hop in her step.

Creating and decorating her booth, adding to the ambiance and environment of Green Hills coming together, and visiting with friends she didn't see often enough put her in a wonderful mood.

Finding one Theodore Gwenn cooking at her stove did not.

"Why are you here?" she asked, stopping in her tracks on the bottom step.

"Good morning," Teddy replied, eyes gleaming and silly smile in place.

"How'd you get in the house?"

"Are you hungry?" he countered.

"What are you doing?"

"Making breakfast," he said, his tone indicating she should've been able to figure that out for herself. "Do you prefer your eggs scrambled or fried?"

"Neither, I—"

"Oh, grab those toasties from the oven for me, please," he interrupted.

Baylin frowned at the back of his head, but she did as he asked…only because burnt toast equaled wasted bread and a stinky kitchen.

Coffee Monday, a full breakfast Tuesday. What in the world would Wednesday bring?

Nothing. Wednesday will bring nothing. It will simply be one day closer to the day he leaves.

Baylin pulled the cookie sheet from the oven, set it on a quilted hot pad on the table, and walked to the pantry for a new jar of blackberry jam. If she had to eat breakfast, she might as well enjoy it.

"Fried it is," Teddy announced as he cracked an egg in a skillet. "They're my specialty. Is sunny side up okay?"

"Fine," Baylin said, giving in. "Why are you cooking breakfast in my kitchen at the crack of dawn?"

"Because you cooked for me."

He said it so matter of fact, as if that made all the sense in the world.

"I cooked for myself and just happened to have enough for you, too," Baylin argued. Was she trying to convince herself, perhaps?

"Two nights in a row," Teddy added, less matter of fact and much more *I see right through you.*

"Yes, well...you'd earned a decent dinner for all the work you helped me do leading up to those meals."

"Of course."

He might as well have said *Whatever you say, dear...*in the world's most placating tone.

Rather than respond, Baylin set the table for two.

The bacon smelled very good, and her stomach growled.

She poured two cups of coffee, added sugar and cream to one for herself and left the other black and bitter for Teddy, and put them at their places just as Teddy declared, "Breakfast is served."

I'd sooo like to wipe that victorious smile from his face.

But Teddy hadn't lied about the eggs...delicious. And the bacon? Even better than it smelled.

Her coffee tasted like ambrosia, and the buttery toasted dinner roll — leftover from their dinner the night before — with a dollop of homemade blackberry jam, gave the morning a sweet start.

In fact, it set the tone for the entire day.

They worked side-by-side...feeding and watering animals, gathering the day's eggs, repairing damaged boards on the pigpen, and cleaning out the barn stalls. Teddy chopped firewood while Baylin piled extra hay and straw in various places for added insulation against the wintry nights.

Baylin begged him to take a break, to leave her alone to do her work in hopes she might catch up on her list. She provided every excuse she could think of to get him out of her hair, but Teddy ignored her pleas. He never hesitated in the slightest to chip in, never balked at the grossness of mucking animal waste.

Nor did Teddy stop talking and smiling. No matter how dirty the job or how menial the task, his litany of questions, curiosity, songs, and stories continued.

His tales were generic, detailed enough that Baylin got the gist of his personality and quirks, but not so much that she could tell where he'd grown up and what his childhood had been like. She still didn't know how he'd come into the fancy sports car, how he managed to have endless days off work, or where he was headed when he found himself stranded for Valentine's Day in Green Hills, Oklahoma.

As the hours passed, his eternal sunshine and good mood stopped driving Baylin so crazy. After lunch, his silly songs became entertaining. His jabbering made the time pass and the work more enjoyable than when she did so much on her own.

Baylin taught Teddy how to cut, roll, and tag fat quarters of quilting fabric for her booth. His attention to detail and accuracy surprised her. He proved to be a quick study when she showed him how to package soaps and attach labels for each scented variety.

"Can I help with your quilt?" Teddy asked when they settled in the parlor after they'd cooked, eaten, and cleaned up their dinner.

"I'm pretty much finished with it…just in time to submit it for judging," Baylin answered, astonished she'd be delivering it to the Busy Bees' Quilt Guild on Wednesday.

"It's beautiful; you're going to win."

Again with the blatant, matter of fact confidence.

If only I had a fraction of that certainty.

"I doubt it. Our local guild and sewing groups are full of quilters accomplished far beyond my skill level."

"But this design is so unique. It catches your eye and fills your heart… It boasts *I'm not afraid to shout my love from the mountaintops!* A real showstopper… I think it's perfect. Definitely a winner."

His praise filled Baylin with hope. She didn't stand a chance, not with Sadie Jones's immaculate piecing which produced perfect joints and never nipped a point, or Judge

Dorothy Roberts's exquisite appliqué that couldn't be matched, or Maree Davenport's lovely fabrics, designed right in her shop on Main Street and then sold all over the world.

But Teddy's pep talk encouraged Baylin to be proud of what she'd accomplished.

"Thank you," she said with earnest appreciation.

Baylin smiled at him…an actual smile, void of the distance and barriers she'd tried in vain to maintain. It was a smile straight from her heart.

10

The beauty of caring for seniors
is realizing that they are heroes
in their own right.
Karen Clark

I'm growing on her!

Boy howdy, if that thought didn't put a skip in Teddy's step as he climbed from Baylin's truck to deliver her quilt to the guild ladies in town.

She'd hesitated after breakfast Wednesday morning, resisting when he'd offered to drive her quilt into town so she could begin working on the gazillion cookies she planned on baking and decorating over the next two days.

Teddy had persisted.

He'd also convinced her to decorate one out of every three cookies, packaging two unfrosted cookies behind a fancy iced one because, truly, didn't everyone like plain shortbreads best?

If Baylin didn't make a few allowances, she'd never get to everything she intended to get done. She'd never have a free minute, never find time to relax, take an evening off, perhaps even pause for a full day…maybe for a baseball game or a road trip or something.

Baylin might not *like* him, not in the way he'd fallen for her, but she would learn to stop and smell the roses a little before he headed out. On that score, Teddy wouldn't take no for an answer.

She worked too hard, did too much. If she didn't slow down a little, life was going to pass her by. Then somewhere down the road, she'd regret not being present on her own journey, not enjoying it more along the way. But by then it would be too late. Teddy couldn't imagine anything worse than that amazing woman settling for mere contentment. She deserved a life that balanced the farm she loved and the chores she excelled at doing, with time to rest and relax and laugh, a life bursting with joy and happiness…one without regrets.

"Who are you?" a crotchety older woman snapped at Teddy the moment he walked into the church's fellowship hall. "And why do you have Baylin's quilt?" she barked.

"Mrs. Jones?" Teddy asked, afraid the lady would answer *yes*.

"Thank the good Lord, no," she answered with a tone of haughty disdain. "Do I look like a do-gooder up in everyone's business?"

Teddy had no answer.

"That's *exactly* what you look like, Dottie," another elderly woman offered, entering the room from the kitchen along the back wall. "And you sound like it, too," she added. "I'm Mrs. Jones," she continued, smiling kindly in Teddy's direction. "Call me Miss Sadie. You ignore Dot—Judge Roberts."

"The appliqué genius," Teddy interjected, remembering what Baylin had told him about the talented quilters in the Green Hills area.

"Let's keep that to ourselves," Miss Sadie whispered. "She woke up on the wrong side of the bed…back in 1952, and she hasn't snapped out of it *yet*." She flashed a sly wink at Teddy. "Now, let's see this quilt. Baylin's worked on it for months."

"That's how she works on everything she does," Teddy agreed, unfolding the quilt, careful that it didn't touch the floor.

"Quite true, young man." Miss Sadie brought her palms together, like prayer hands at her heart, as she leaned forward to examine Baylin's work. "Ooh," she gasped. "It's incredible," she praised. "Dottie, come look," she called out without taking her eyes from the quilt. "She managed at least a dozen stitches per inch…amazing."

"And it's her first quilt to enter in a contest," Teddy added, just to make sure these ladies realized *how* amazing it — *she* — was.

"Yes," Miss Sadie said. She glanced up at Teddy with a gleam in her eye. "And it's very kind of you to bring her quilt in for judging. It's not like Baylin to delegate; I can only imagine how many irons she must be juggling in the fire today."

The way Miss Sadie *oohed* and *ahhed* over Baylin's quilt endeared the sweeter of the two ladies to Teddy. When she blended her idioms in Baylin's defense, Teddy fought the urge to give her a big ol' bear hug.

For propriety's sake, he settled with giving her a big ol' smile instead, and he offered to help the women hang the quilts they were organizing when he arrived.

A few other volunteers cycled through, but for the most part, Teddy assisted Miss Sadie and Judge Roberts. The ladies kept him very busy, and the time passed in the blink of an eye…

They directed Teddy to position heavy metal bases for the pipe-and-drape system they'd rented from a company in Dallas to serve as frames for hanging the quilts. Teddy couldn't believe the delivery crew had dropped off the parts without lending a hand to set up.

Then Miss Sadie requested all hands on deck, and everyone worked together to assemble the uprights and drapery bars. Luckily, they had enough ladders on hand to work in pairs hanging the black event drapes. When they'd finished that step, Miss Sadie, Judge Roberts, and the other guild committee members brought out the quilts for display.

Stepping off the ladder after hanging the final quilt three hours later, Teddy took a moment to marvel at the art exhibit they'd created.

Baylin hadn't exaggerated when she said the local quilters were talented artists. The variety of quilt styles, the intricate patterns, the pairings of fabric colors and prints, and the workmanship displayed astounded Teddy.

Baylin's was by far the prettiest, but there were some remarkable quilts to behold everywhere he looked.

"Are all quilt shows so magnificent?" he wondered aloud.

"Oh yes," Miss Sadie answered; at the exact same moment Judge Roberts mumbled, "Not by a long shot."

Teddy chuckled at the two friends, as different in personality as night and day, but both adorable and passionate about showing off the masterpieces displayed throughout the church's large fellowship hall, vast sanctuary, and wide corridors.

"What happens when you outgrow the church?"

A shadow of sadness fell over both ladies' faces, putting Teddy on high alert.

"It used to be much bigger," Judge Roberts said with a deep frown.

"And it will be again," Miss Sadie added, patting her friend's shoulder in encouragement.

They explained that in the past the town had hosted festivals and events like the quilt show at the city park, but a terrible explosion the year before had destroyed the recreation center. The devastation left the community without a building large enough to house the number of quilts they had accepted in the contest before the tragedy.

Miss Sadie and Judge Roberts stood close together, even wrapping an arm around one another for support. They both wiped tears from their eyes by the end of their story.

"I'm sorry for bringing up bad memories," Teddy said.

"Tough times produce tough people," Judge Roberts said, dismissing his apology. "Takes more than a gang of thugs to destroy this town."

"Hardships and challenges are part of every story, an *important* part of our history," Miss Sadie said, pinning Teddy with an uncanny look of omniscient power. "There's not a single one of us who's not been affected *and strengthened* by the struggles we've been through."

Teddy nodded in agreement, finished folding the ladder, and helped hide the tools and supplies they'd been using in the church kitchen, where they'd be out of sight during the show. He said his goodbyes and made his way out of town on County Road 214, heading toward O'Casey Farm.

As he drove, Miss Sadie's nugget of wisdom rattled around in his thoughts. Had she seen into Teddy's history, or was she hinting at someone else's story?

Baylin's perhaps?

Judge Roberts had dropped cryptic messages under her breath on multiple occasions throughout the afternoon, always when Miss Sadie couldn't hear…things like, *Quilts won't be the only competition at this Valentine's Day festival,* and …*town's in for an entertaining weekend, I reckon.*

She'd scared him a bit with her response when Miss Sadie had asked if Baylin knew who Teddy was…who he *really* was. It hadn't occurred to him that Baylin *didn't* know. Even if she didn't follow baseball, she had Internet service at the farm and had surely searched his name for a minimal background check.

But when he said as much to Miss Sadie, Judge Roberts cackled — *cackled* — at Teddy before declaring, *This oughta be good,* and continued laughing as she walked away looking the happiest she'd been all day.

Teddy left out that part of the story when he returned to the farmhouse, eager to tell Baylin about his time in town. He found her in the kitchen, right where he'd left her hours earlier. She kept right on working while he recapped his day.

"They're always a hoot," she laughed, shaking her head at the women's antics. "There's a tribe of ladies in Green Hills that run the place. As you can imagine, those two lead the pack."

"I don't doubt that for a second! They're pretty great," he said.

"The best," Baylin agreed. "They've taught me so much."

"About quilting?"

"About life."

When she didn't expound, Teddy thought it best to switch gears. Miss Sadie's declaration hit a little too close to home, and Teddy didn't want his conversation with Baylin to take a turn toward anything sad or dark.

"What's the plan for the seven thousand cookies you baked while I was gone?" he teased.

"Only six hundred eighty-four. The last thirty-six are in the ovens."

"Sixty dozen… That's a lot of cookies!"

"Only ten dozen more than I made last year, and I sold out on the first day of the festival. This year, I'm making more and adding frosting—"

"To a third of them," Teddy interrupted, reminding Baylin of his idea she'd agreed to earlier.

"*To a third of them,*" Baylin acquiesced. "That way I can charge more without disappointing anyone."

"I can't imagine you ever disappointing anyone."

"You might be surprised," Baylin replied with a sardonic smirk while mixing icing colors in glass bowls. "But not with cookies. Those seem to please pretty much everyone. Plus," she added, "my friend, Anita, just bought a food truck and is fixing it up as a dessert shack. She rented booth space to give people a taste of what she'll be selling when the truck is up and running."

"Anita? Would I have met her today at the church?"

"I doubt it."

Baylin spoke with abandon, albeit about someone besides herself. Teddy listened with rapt attention. Happy as a lark, he'd continue doing so as long as she kept talking, sharing her world, and letting him carry a tiny fraction of the load.

"Between cooking for the Sharps, helping her mom clean houses, and baking at Triple T's on the weekends, she can't find enough time to work on her truck, much less quilt or volunteer."

"You went to school together?"

"I'm a few years older than Anita, but it's a small town," Baylin said with a shrug. "We've known each other our entire lives, have always gone to church together, and attended several volleyball camps together when we were kids."

"Will her dessert shack be any good?"

"It'll be amazing. Anita's a magician in the kitchen."

"You don't worry about the competition?"

"Not at all," Baylin said without hesitation. "I don't mind baking and cooking if there's a demand for it and if I can make a little money from selling what I make. But I don't feel called to be in the kitchen; that's not my passion."

She said it was such finality that Teddy again maneuvered the conversation to shallower waters.

"And what's a triple *T*?"

"A three-toed turtle."

"Is that a real thing?" he asked, managing a straight face.

She stopped stirring food coloring into mixing bowls at the speed of a Formula One race car to look at him as though he'd grown a second head.

"*Is that a real thing?*" she repeated, eyes wide with mocking drama. "Of course three-toed turtles are real. They appear a bit boring or drab on the outside, but they're quite resilient, living to a ripe, old age of seventy — or older — and ridding eastern Oklahoma of hundreds of thousands of insects throughout their lifespan."

Smart and snooty Baylin might've been the most fun version of her Teddy'd seen so far.

Her smile and silliness did strange things to his equilibrium. And he liked it.

"I'm now educated," he said, lifting his hands in defeat. "Thank you," he said, bringing his palms together in a gesture of gratitude. "I feel better knowing all there is to know about a triple *T*."

She rolled sassy brown eyes at him and returned to coloring icing.

"Any chance I'll get to meet a three-toed turtle while I'm here?"

"Not likely this time of year," she answered. "But if you come back later in the spring, I guarantee you'll see plenty. And in the meantime, we can have dinner at The Triple T diner in town...best burger and milkshake in a three-hour radius."

"Now *that* sounds like a date."

11

———

***Well, I think we tried very hard
not to be overconfident,
because when you get overconfident,
that's when something snaps up and bites you.***
Neil Armstrong

He was only teasing — *surely* — but Baylin's cheeks burned red hot, nonetheless.

Teddy must've noticed. The gleam in his pale green eyes became even shinier.

"Grab an apron from the back of the pantry door; I'd hate for you to ruin your fifth baseball t-shirt in as many days as you've been here."

"These are the height of fashion, I'll have you know," Teddy replied, running his hands over the silly peanut dressed as a vintage umpire emblazoned on his chest, which meant the muscles under said t-shirt became clearly visible through the soft cotton material.

Good heavens.

"Do you ever wear anything besides goofy mascots no one has heard of?"

"Ouch. Shots fired!" Teddy clutched his chest. "I better get that apron so I don't bleed all over the floor."

He returned before she'd adequately re-centered her nerves, but she could fake confidence with the best of 'em.

"Ready to flood?" she asked.

"Sure?" he questioned.

Baylin raised an eyebrow at his first *ever* sign of uncertainty.

"Sure," he repeated with a definitive dip of his chin.

"It's very easy," she told him. "I'll pipe an outline of frosting along the edge of each cookie. Give it a minute to dry and then use the matching icing to fill in, or *flood*, the top. They'll dry overnight, and I'll add a message to each heart in the morning."

"Like those little boxes of Valentine's candy," Teddy exclaimed.

"Conversation Hearts… It's the theme of this year's festival."

"Which explains why you named your quilt *Speaking of Love*," he filled in.

"Not too original, I guess," Baylin said with a slight shrug.

"But it is," he countered. She gestured to brush off his contradiction, but Teddy circled the kitchen island, took the icing bag from her hand, and laid it on their workspace. Taking hold of her shoulders, he turned Baylin to face him.

"You were right about the quality of the quilts in the show," Teddy told her, looking directly into her eyes. A warm wave of awareness skittered down her spine. "But yours is special… unique, bolder. It grabs your attention and refuses to let go, daring anyone who sees it to walk away. The hearts in their shades of deep reds and hot pinks scream strength while your elaborate stitching design with white thread on white fabric promises soft femininity." He searched her eyes before lifting a hand from her shoulder to her cheek. "Incomparable," he whispered, cupping her jaw and caressing her skin with his thumb.

Teddy made it difficult to inhale and exhale like a regular human being.

Because he made her feel like something far beyond normal.

"Thank you." She met his gaze, determined to match his conviction…fake it 'til you make it and all that rubbish.

Teddy studied her for another long moment. He gave a single nod as his beautiful lips bloomed into that smile that never seemed too far away.

"So, what words of love do you have planned for us?"

"Excuse me?"

"For the cookies," he said, as though *she* needed to keep up. "What are we writing on them? How about *Hey, hottie!* Ooo, or maybe *How U Doin?*"

His over-the-top drama proved her undoing; she gave into the urge to laugh, and then she — *they* — couldn't stop.

By the time they'd outlined and flooded the two hundred forty cookies she'd set out to decorate, they'd both passed into goofy delirium and found every little thing hilarious.

Lying in bed later than night, Baylin predicted her abs would be sore from laughing so hard through the afternoon and evening. Teddy had teased and joked and entertained, and Baylin had dished out equal banter in return.

They'd had fun.

Teddy is fun.

He delighted in everything he did. He made working side-by-side enjoyable.

And while Teddy never complained about the workload, he finagled Baylin into eating breakfast and sharing cups of coffee each morning and stopping for lunch — seated at the kitchen table instead of her normal sandwich on the go — every afternoon. He forced her to slow down, to pay more attention to the world around her…things like spending extra time grooming the horses and feeding the other animals, chatting all the while because, as Teddy put it, *They thrive on conversation, too.*

Best of all, in the evenings, he never left her side…begging for basic jobs to help cook dinner, demanding she let him wash and dry and put away the dishes while she sat at the kitchen table, tending to paperwork on her laptop. Then they'd move into the parlor, where Teddy would con Baylin into setting aside her computer or bills or spiral full of chores and tasks and obligations. She'd work on her quilt projects while he read or watched sports on TV.

Those were the only moments Teddy grew quiet, yet their silence never grew awkward or strained. In three short days, they'd settled into a routine together, a peaceful, happy, and all too domestic one.

"He might not be all *that* bad," Baylin said to the mirror late Thursday afternoon. They'd spent the entire morning writing words and phrases on the decorated cookies and packaging them in treat bags with Valentine tags and satin ribbon bows. Teddy had been a huge help. "But he's not staying, either."

She reminded herself of that fact no less than a thousand times each day, and she'd put the mantra on a continuous loop in her mind while she'd showered and dressed for the Valentine's Dance, a pre-party to the Sweetheart Festival.

"Let's get this thing over with," Baylin said, still talking to her reflection. She exhaled a deep breath and applied Strawberry Shock lipstick with a swipe of shiny gloss on top. She fluffed her long, loose waves and finished with a hairspray fly-by. Then Baylin adjusted the belt of her long-sleeved wrap dress, stepped into and zipped up knee-high, nude-colored patent leather boots, and headed downstairs to fetch her favorite winter coat: a fantastic, long, vintage-styled, fit-and-flare sheepskin shearling coat in cognac brown, complete with a luxurious hooded collar that folded down into a dramatic lapel, which kept her very warm in addition to looking fabulous.

Hands down, getting dressed up was the best part of the many community dances, banquets, and fundraisers held in Green Hills throughout the year. She loved socializing with friends at those events, of course, but Baylin hung out with them on a regular basis, and ninety-nine percent of the time they wore jeans, a t-shirt or flannel, and their oldest, most comfortable pair of tennis shoes. No, for Baylin, donning a magnificent dress, killer stilettos, and fur-lined *haute couture* jacket was for herself…one hundred percent self-indulgent and pure fun.

An appreciative whistle reached Baylin before she'd descended the stairs enough to see the source of the catcalling. When he came into sight, her heart skipped a beat.

Teddy Gwenn cleaned up well…too well.

"You just happened to have a suit in your duffel bag?"

To her pleasant surprise, Baylin's voice didn't betray the quiver she felt.

"Not exactly," he answered with a guilty grin. "I found a men's shop in town yesterday."

"Henry's," Baylin said. "It's been a staple in Green Hills since the 1940s."

"The owner, Elijah Davis— What a nice guy! He and his daughter helped me pick this out." Teddy crossed one foot over the other and performed a rather debonaire spin to show off his new clothes. "Not bad, huh?"

"It'll do," Baylin allowed, sweeping past him to get her coat, determined to *not* let on just how *not bad* Teddy looked.

The Davis family — with the exception of Daniel, who graduated from Green Hills High School when Baylin had been in junior high, but whom everyone in their small town knew and loved, abandoned the family trade to become a fireman — carried the reputation of being excellent clothiers, and Elijah was particularly famous for knowing how to make a body look its best. They'd surpassed their own high standard in dressing Teddy.

"I appreciate them working with me on zero notice to pick out something I can use a lot down the road. I mean, this suit is perfect...fits me to a tee."

That it does.

Elijah and Jessica must've squealed with delight when they saw him walk into the store.

Brown herringbone fabric, a classy yet casual hue, almost walnut in color, looked to be high quality, which meant it wasn't inexpensive, was a perfect choice to complement the traditional, two-button coat style and trendy but polished, slim cut. His tie and pocket square — a playful design of flowers and birds in vibrant shades of reds, bright canary yellow, and soothing browns on a warm, peachy-coral background — mimicked Teddy's peppy yet stable disposition. The rich whiskey-colored leather, lace-up dress shoes added an elegant, dapper element to the ensemble. Together, the new pieces of his wardrobe teamed up to create something one hundred percent *Teddy*: unique, effective, and eye-catching. One could toss in *heart-stopping* for good measure...if one was so inclined.

Hope you're ready, Cupid. It's going to be a busy night...

Teddy Gwenn would be quite a hit at the Valentine's Dance.

"What do you call this?" Teddy asked, pointing a finger at Baylin's outfit with an admiring eye.

"A dress?"

"That's not *just* a dress," Teddy replied before helping her slip on her coat. "What color would you call that?"

"Red?"

"To say you are beautiful in that *red dress* is the understatement of the year."

"The year's still young," she argued. Baylin punctuated her clipped rebuttal by pushing Teddy out the door, locking it, and proceeding to her truck.

"I'm searching for better adjectives, ones that more accurately paint the picture you make…an image I won't soon forget. Can't you help me just a little?"

Teddy opened the driver's side door for her and held out a hand to help her up…debonair *and* a gentleman. Great.

Instead of climbing in, Baylin pressed the keys into his open palm.

"These heels aren't made for driving," she explained, walking around the cab to the passenger's side. Teddy followed.

Of course he did. And extended his hand as he'd done before.

The urge to be persnickety surged in Baylin's veins. Teddy got his way too often, winning every tug-of-war they fought. Baylin needed to win a few rounds to even the score.

In the end, though, she relented. She grasped his strong, warm hand and stepped on the running board to settle into her seat.

"But they *are* impressive," Teddy said, eyeing her boots, one eyebrow waggling while his lips lifted in a suggestive yet playful grin.

She shook her head as he closed her door and hurried around the bed of the truck.

His unflagging and light-hearted demeanor weakened Baylin's resolve to see their night as a responsibility to the community instead of a potential date with a drop-dead gorgeous guy she had no business fancying.

"Geranium," she said, riding along the highway leading into Green Hills.

He cast a confused expression her way.

"I'd call this shade of red *geranium*, not as yellow as orange and not as pink as salmon. It's a DVF…Diane Von Furstenberg. She's a fashion genius and a cultural icon. You should read about her sometime; her story's incredible, impactful, and inspiring. I dreamed of owning one of her dresses for years. Then, I saw this one in an ad last year, and I couldn't get it out of my mind."

"I can relate." Teddy glanced over to flash a look of teasing commiseration.

Baylin displayed an annoyed look at his silliness. In reality, the compliments meant a lot, far more than the flirting. Despite his easy-going disposition, his perpetual loquaciousness, and his permanent smile, Baylin didn't take Teddy for someone who'd lie…not even about something as silly as saying she looked nice. If he didn't mean it, he wouldn't have said it.

"I hate spending money on things that don't benefit the farm, but this dress— well, I just went for it."

"I, for one, am glad you did." His voice dropped deeper and his smile softened as he looked her way. "And you *should* treat yourself now and then," he said. "You work way too hard as it is. I've only been around a few days, and I can unequivocally attest to that. You deserve to pamper yourself, take a break now and then…you know, stop to smell the roses."

"I do love flowers," she conceded, gazing out the window.

"What's in the boxes?" he asked a few miles down the road.

"Hm?" Her attention had wandered to intentions and plans and hopes and dreams she'd set aside years before, when Papa Joe died and someone had to step up as farm manager. If she hadn't, her family would have lost their land, their business, and their legacy. In another life, though, perhaps the sweet scent of flowers in bloom would've filled her days.

"I notice you loaded a bunch of stuff into the truck after I went to the barn to shower. I would've done that for you." He pinned her with a knowing look.

"I'm sure you would have, but I didn't need any help. I did it just fine myself."

"Hmph," Teddy grunted. Baylin grinned. The inelegance of the noise juxtaposed with the suave figure driving her three-quarter ton farm truck humored Baylin.

His contradictions kept her guessing. Fancy sports car versus faded jeans and five-and-dime t-shirts; high-end cowboy boots that bore the scuffed marks of age and use; the intense determination to work but no apparent job; his talent for active listening while talking... The desire to explore the paradoxical facets of Teddy's personality tugged at Baylin, growing stronger every hour they spent together.

Keep it casual, she reminded herself. *Keep it safe.*

"Popcorn," she said, earning herself another cute puppy dog eyes look of bewilderment. "The boxes don't weigh a thing because they're filled with bags of white chocolate popcorn. I made and bagged them right after you left for town yesterday, while the sugar cookie dough chilled in the fridge. They're my contribution to the refreshment table tonight."

"Popcorn, huh?" Teddy paused before flashing a warm smile at Baylin, the one that always sent her pulse into over-drive. Afraid her voice might reveal too much, she only nodded in response. "In that case, I guess I'm not offended you didn't ask for my help. And I know which dessert I'll choose first. But don't even think about unloading those boxes when we get there. I've got 'em! There'll be no buts about it."

"We'll see." Baylin lifted one shoulder to feign indifference. *Yes, we'll see.*

12

———

"The Lady in Red"
Song written and performed by
Chris de Burgh (1986)

They compromised.

Teddy grabbed two boxes and a large trough-like bucket, leaving one box of popcorn for Baylin to carry into the high school gym.

She arranged the clear cellophane snack bags — which she'd tied with skinny strips of fabric matching the colors and prints he'd seen in her quilt — in the galvanized-metal tub. While he carried the empty boxes out to the truck, Baylin went to hang her coat on a temporary rack set out in the gymnasium foyer.

When he returned, he spotted her across the basketball court-turned-dance floor. She had no clue how incredible she looked, no idea how she lit up a room.

Teddy knew. The ever-present warm, thrumming weight in his chest refused to let him ignore or forget the effect Baylin had on him.

The sensation cooled a few degrees when a guy — tall, athletic build — led her to dance under the strobe lights and disco balls hanging from the rafters.

"That youngest Crockett boy is quite a looker," a none-too-sweet voice scratched in Teddy's ear. "Been chasing after Baylin since I had them both in the preschool Bible class at church…years and years ago." She emphasized the *years and years*.

"Good evening, Judge Roberts," he said, granting the ol' biddy his most gracious expression. "Miss Sadie, it's nice to see you again," Teddy added, facing the second woman with a genuine smile.

"Doesn't the gym look festive?" Miss Sadie asked, waving a hand at the massive balloon arches, the twisted crepe streamers, and the umpteen thousand construction paper hearts dangling above their heads.

Before Teddy could comment, Judge Roberts piped in with a sarcastic grunt, followed by, "It's astonishing how cheap tissue paper jazzes up a place."

"I think it's great," Teddy said. "Reminds me of attending prom at my high school."

"I can just imagine," Judge Roberts weighed in, judgmental sarcasm dripping from every word. "Fancy boy like you and all."

"Ignore her," Miss Sadie said. "If she's breathing, she's instigating," she added with a dismissing wave toward her friend.

"Just testing the waters," Judge Roberts muttered under her breath.

Baylin and her dance partner saved Teddy from having to curate a reasonable response. They finished their dance close to Teddy and his two elderly companions as the deejay transitioned into a new song, stepping away from the crowd of kids taking over the dance floor for an überpopular line dance Teddy also remembered from his own high school days.

Some traditions never die.

"Miss Sadie, Judge... You're both very lovely tonight," Baylin said, hugging the former and bestowing a beautiful smile upon the latter. Slightly out of breath from the upbeat Texas two-step she'd just danced, a warm flush bloomed across her cheeks. Had exertion caused it...or interest in the man at her side? Did Judge Roberts know more about Baylin's love life than Teddy did?

Of course she did.

It was a tiny town, and Teddy'd been there for what amounted to the blink of an eye. Everyone in that building knew more about Baylin, her history, and her boyfriends than Teddy did.

The thought soured his stomach.

"Teddy, this is Michael; a friend from— well, forever," Baylin said. "Michael, this is Teddy; he's renting the barn apartment while Jax repairs his car."

The two men sized up one another, each on one side of Baylin, who didn't seem to notice the ridiculous, testosterone-filled byplay.

Yet another guy, a little shorter than Teddy and Michael approached. He, too, appeared to have a longtime friendship with Baylin.

"Hey, Traise," she exclaimed.

"Happy almost-Valentine's Day," he said, hugging Baylin. "Hi, guys," he added with happy eyes and a jubilant smile. "Come on, let's swing," he said, holding out his hand to Baylin. He didn't waste time with introductions.

Neither did the constant stream of boys, teens, and men of all ages eager to dance with Baylin.

Teddy growled but managed to keep it quiet and to himself.

"Having fun?" Miss Sadie asked, joining Teddy on the edge of the dance floor where he stood brooding. They'd been there two hours, and Baylin had been cutting a rug the entire time… and not with him.

"A blast," he replied. His tone implied the extreme opposite of his answer. "Now I understand what Judge Roberts was warning me about yesterday: every male in town is in love with her."

"Just in *like*," Miss Sadie said. Her kind voice drew his attention away from the object of their discussion, the woman in red from whom he couldn't seem to look away. "Baylin's special. But you already know that."

"And they don't?"

"Oh, I'm sure they'd each welcome a chance to take her on a date…to dinner or a movie a time or two. Who wouldn't? Baylin's smart and funny and strong and independent. And she's stunningly gorgeous," she added with a sparkle in her eye. "She could've snagged any of those potential suitors anytime she wanted. Baylin's holding out for someone who wants more than that, for someone who sees more than that when they look her way."

Miss Sadie let that sink in while the two of them watched Baylin, another nameless fellow, and half of Green Hills twirl and prance to the music.

"What do *you* see?" she asked. But she didn't wait for an answer before calling out to a friend and moving on to her next conversation.

One thing Teddy did not want to see for another second was Baylin in that guy's arms.

He found a trash can for his lemonade cup and made his way to the center of the dancing throng. As he reached Baylin, the deejay took the tempo down several notches.

Her back was to him, so Teddy leaned down to whisper in her ear.

"Let's dance."

His hand came to the small of her back. As she turned toward him, Baylin twirled into his chest. Teddy lifted her arms to his shoulders and held her close.

They danced just like that, with Baylin's cheek laying against Teddy's heart and Teddy's cheek resting on the crown of her head. He luxuriated in the silky feel of her hair and the intoxicating scent of her perfume.

As that song ended, another began, and Teddy never released Baylin.

The third song— maybe the fourth… Teddy had lost count. Whatever the number, it moved at a quicker pace. He ignored the tempo for a moment, reluctant to loosen their embrace. Then, as the tune reached its chorus, Teddy lifted his head and took one of her hands, adopting a closed partners position typical to ballroom dancing. She giggled at his quick switch to such a formal posture. Then she giggled with glee as Teddy answered with a wink and led her into a traditional foxtrot.

They skipped and swooped and flowed around the floor. Teddy maneuvered them around other couples, maintaining the lock his eyes held with hers.

Yes, Miss Sadie, I see her. And I desire her in every way. I'm pretty certain I already love her.

Instead of making him falter, the acknowledgement bolstered Teddy's confidence to new heights. Those other guys had been around, wasting time and missing their chances…not Teddy's problem.

It was his turn to show Baylin what love could be.

13
_____

Coming together is a beginning;
keeping together is progress;
working together is success.
Edward Everett Hale

aylin's nerves tingled and her heart filled with hope on the drive home from the Valentine's Dance.

Best one ever.

Teddy in that suit, the way he watched her all night long…

Yes, she'd noticed.

His signature smile had turned so grave that no one had even approached him to talk or dance the entire night, which was saying a lot in Green Hills, where a newcomer attracted lots of attention and a young, good-looking newcomer set the proverbial grapevine on fire.

The more she had enjoyed herself, dancing and chatting with friends, the more ominous his countenance had become. She'd delighted in every second.

But then he'd had enough, had stepped in to claim his dance…to claim her heart.

She looked at him across the cab of the truck and couldn't stop her lips from lifting into a knowing smile. He glanced over and smiled right back. An air of possibilities and promise zapped all around them.

"What's the agenda for tomorrow?" Teddy asked. "I'm guessing it'll be a long day with the festival beginning."

"Very," she corrected. "Booth set up begins at nine in the morning, so I need to load the trailer between six and seven o'clock. I'll feed the animals and check water levels before then. The festival technically begins at three, but they don't open the exhibit doors until after the baseball game. I hired a few high school kids I know from church to help me cover the booth throughout the weekend. Mostly, though, I like to be there to oversee things and answer questions shoppers have. You don't have to—" Baylin stopped talking when she noticed the look on Teddy's face.

In the dark, she'd missed his expression of wonderment, joy, and interest at the mention of his favorite sport.

"Yes?" she asked.

"Baseball game?"

"Oh, yeah. I guess I forgot to mention it. Schools and businesses close early for the unofficial festival kickoff: a six-inning sandlot baseball game at the park."

"Who gets to play in it?"

"Anyone who wants to, I suppose."

"Are you playing in it?"

"I usually cover a spot in the outfield for an inning or two, if they need me."

"Who is *they?* Who gets to pick the teams? Do they have equipment? And who umpires?"

"Easy now," Baylin teased. "It's just a fun little pickup game. No one cares about the teams and the score and stuff."

"Yeah, right," Teddy joked. "Who are the coaches? That'll tell me all I need to know."

"The chiefs," she answered. "Miles Everett, the fire chief, coaches one team, and his best friend, Stanley Crockett, the police chief, coaches the other. You met his son tonight…Michael."

"Will he be playing?"

"I'm sure he will if he's not on shift," Baylin said. "He's a police officer, just like his three big brothers. In fact, their entire family is in law enforcement, even aunts and uncles. They're a great family."

"You know a lot about them."

"Michael and I were born six days apart, right here in Green Hills. There's no way I could *not* know a lot about them," she laughed.

"Do you play on his team or the fire team?"

"It changes from year to year, but Chief Everett got to me first, so I'm with the GHFD this time."

They'd reached the farm and the garage; fatigue had set in. Baylin's pajamas were calling her name.

"The dance was fun," she told Teddy at her kitchen door. "I'm glad you were here."

"Thanks," Teddy said, unlocking the door and handing Baylin her keys. "It was." He studied her face, a slight smile on his inviting lips. They'd be warm to the touch, gentle and very kissable. "And thank you for the dance," he said, running his fingers down her cheek. His voice had dropped, grown husky.

Baylin held her breath, wondering if — *hoping that* — he'd lean down and kiss her.

He didn't.

After one last long look, he retreated to the barn.

Opportunity missed or disaster averted? If only she knew.

*F*our a.m. came early.

By five, she'd showered, dressed for the day, and started a pot of coffee.

Layering up to ward off the predawn chill, Baylin stepped out the back door to find Teddy in the chicken coop.

"What are you doing?"

"Checking for eggs," he answered. "None today… Despite the heat lamps, I think it's too cold out."

"I mean, what are you doing awake? It's insanely early."

"You're up."

"I don't have a choice," she argued.

"Maybe I don't want a choice." He tossed it out there like the mystery message meant nothing. But what was Baylin supposed to make of it? Was he saying he'd like to stay? At the farm? With her?

She'd had too little sleep, the hour was too early, and the list in her pocket was way too extensive to exert energy dissecting his cryptic statement, but it stayed with her all morning long.

As they fed and watered the horses, Baylin considered how comfortable he'd become in her domain. When he offered to hitch up the cargo trailer to the truck, she noted how nice it was to have his capable help around the farm. And when he saw her flower arrangements, his praise and admiration made her heart soar…

"We've got produce crates, the soap and fabric bins, the candles, the home decor tubs, the canned goods, the cookie boxes, the farm t-shirts, two round racks of all the other clothing stuff, stationary junk, and these O'Casey Farm banners and signs. Are we missing anything?" Teddy asked.

"Just one last thing," Baylin said. "In the downstairs guest room."

Teddy followed her back into the house and down the hall.

When she opened the door to the bedroom, Teddy looked over her head and stopped dead in his tracks.

"I can't figure out if it's a green room, a jungle, or a flower shop," he exclaimed.

"A bit of all three, I suppose," Baylin said. "I took the furniture out a few years ago, so I had a good place to put my potted plants over the winter. This room gets the best sunlight since it faces the east. It seemed like a better use of the square footage, since I have plenty of beds for guests upstairs."

"And in the barn," he quipped.

"Yes, for the riff-raff," she razzed.

He responded with a dramatic display of faux indignation, but his attention stayed on the multitude of flower arrangements, some made of silk and others made of dried flowers, covering every inch of the room.

"You made these?"

Baylin's pulse quickened. Why did sharing a secret passion — a silly hobby, really — make one feel vulnerable and small?

"Yes," she answered, her voice faint. She'd used a plethora of containers ranging from antique tea pots to wooden bowls to metal tins to crystal cut vases. She'd poured her soul into each of them, desperate to create unique works of art that would bring beauty and joy to their new homes.

"Baylin, they're magnificent." He stopped to catch her eye. "Seriously, these are exquisite. When did you create them?"

"I've been working on them for months. I thought about taking them to the holiday festival on Christmas Eve, but I chickened out."

"Chickened out? Whatever for? These will sell like hotcakes…and for a lot of money."

"I hope so," Baylin admitted, not sharing in his certainty.

They loaded the arrangements, and with all her wares loaded into the truck and trailer, they made their way to the exhibit hall in the Conrad Hotel.

The oldest, most exclusive hotel in town rolled out the red carpet for big events. Her thirty-foot by thirty-foot booth space included display shelving, large tables, lighting, and electricity. All Baylin had to do was drape the raw wood fixtures and transport inside everything from the parking lot.

It sounded easy, but it required a lot of manpower.

And my God will supply every need of yours according to his riches in glory in Christ Jesus.

Philippians 4:19 popped into Baylin's mind. Teddy had proved to be a godsend.

They worked at a steady pace for hours.

When Baylin stood back to determine what needed to be adjusted, tears sprang to her eyes. Her projects, each one a reflection of her creativity and determination, looked interesting and inviting…amazing, really, layered and staged and displayed in their best light.

"I'm too hungry for tears," Teddy said, wrapping his arm around her shoulder and pulling her in for a comforting hug. "I believe you mentioned turtle burgers the other day?"

"Not turtle burgers," she said, elbowing him in the ribs. "Burgers at The Three-Toed Turtle."

"Can we go? What about the booth?"

"It'll be fine, and as soon as all the vendors finish setting up, they'll lock the doors until this evening. Come on; it's my treat," she offered.

"I'll arm-wrestle you for the bill," he challenged, leading Baylin out of the hotel.

He didn't remove his arm from around her shoulder.

14

The downfall of any leader
in a sport's team is when he gets
carried away with his own ego.
Toto Wolff

An hour later, Teddy considered himself a Triple T's fan. He'd devoured his Sweetheart Special: a double cheeseburger with onions grilled into the meat patties, three slices of cheese — Cheddar, Swiss, and Pepper Jack — and a stack of lettuce, tomato, and pickles sandwiched between layers of mustard and mayonnaise on a homemade bun; an order of onion rings still sizzling from the grease; and a strawberry milkshake served in an icy soda fountain glass, with whipped cream and a cherry on top.

Teddy had finished it off with a fat wedge of chocolate cake, an absolute slice of heaven. Baylin had mentioned a few days earlier that her friend baked at The Three-Toed Turtle on the weekends, so Teddy had asked their server who had baked the dessert. A few minutes later, Anita de la Fuente emerged from the kitchen with a cake box in hand and headed straight for Teddy and Baylin.

"I hear I have a new admirer," she said, setting the box on their table as Baylin rose from her bench seat. The girls shared a hug; it was a treat to watch Baylin light up at seeing her friend.

"For life," Teddy clarified, extending his hand to meet her. "I'm Teddy Gwenn."

"Are you now?" Anita replied, volleying a sly smile back and forth between Teddy and Baylin.

"Baylin mentioned you're a magician when it comes to making desserts; I agree! I've never had a chocolate cake so moist and spongy. And the powdered sugar on top instead of frosting is going to be my favorite forever more."

"Are you sure she didn't say witch instead of magician?" Anita teased, draping an arm around Baylin. "Either way, I'm happy to put my superpowers to good use. I'm glad you enjoyed it."

"Do you have time to sit for a second?" Baylin asked, sliding back into the booth.

"I'd love to. And I boxed up an extra cake for Teddy here to take home…gotta keep the fans happy. Isn't that right slugger?" Baylin moved closer to the wall, and Anita sat beside her.

"Whatever it takes," he said with a laugh. "Thank you! Between your cake, the white chocolate-covered popcorn Baylin made, and my plan to steal a few of her Valentine's cookies from the festival, I can have something sweet after every meal for the rest of the weekend. I feel like a kid on Christmas morning."

"I hated to miss the dance, but I had too much baking left to do… The hotel dining room is packed with food vendors, and I rented a double space."

At Anita's mention of the night before, Teddy's and Baylin's eyes met. A warm glow colored her cheeks; he couldn't look away. In a bold red dress and dazzling high heels or wearing a plaid flannel with jeans and tennis shoes, Baylin captivated and attracted Teddy in an undefinable way. His feelings for her resembled a fastball whizzing down the pipe, high velocity and full of potential. Place the sweet spot of the bat on a ball like that, and he'd blast it 460 feet for a grand slam home run every time. What an experience, one Coach Hayes called life-defining...one for which there existed no defense...one Teddy hoped would never end.

"Hello?" Anita waved a hand between them. "How was it?"

"Fun," Baylin answered.

"Pivotal," Teddy challenged, eyes still glued to Baylin.

"Yes, interesting," Baylin added.

"I've been to a lot of dances around here, and not one of them was interesting and certainly not pivotal," Anita declared. "Who all was there? Karl said he and his brothers couldn't make it; they're down in San Antonio, competing at the stock show and rodeo. I swear, those boys—" She stopped mid-sentence and eyed Teddy and Baylin up and down. Teddy'd been listening... He truly had. But he hadn't given Anita his full attention, which was rude.

"Sorry," he said, dragging his gaze away from Baylin. "I heard people talking about the Sharp triplets while we were hanging quilts at the church Wednesday; they sound both *interesting* and *fun*."

"Crazy and stupid's more like it," Anita said, shaking her head. "Karl promised he'd be around to help me rebuild the engine on the jalopy of a food truck I bought, which was all I could afford. But they had the Breakaway Rodeo Finals in Montana right after Christmas, then the Southwest Expo in Fort Worth until last week. It's always something with cowboys...something pulling them back on a trail to anywhere but here."

"Give him a break," Baylin said as she moved their dishes to clear the space in front of her. She tried, but failed, to conceal a big yawn, folded her arms on the table, and rested her head against them. "You know Karl's sweet on you," she mumbled as her eyes closed.

"Just because you can't be home doesn't mean the people there aren't important," Teddy said, careful to sound neutral rather than defensive or judgy.

"Hard to claim something that doesn't get your attention is a priority," Anita countered with a pointed look at Baylin, whose peaceful, sleeping beauty pierced Teddy's heart.

I could love her so easily.

"Out of sight isn't always out of mind."

"It sure feels like it," Anita said, divulging a thread of insecurity which surprised him as she came across as self-*everything*…reliant, assertive, confident, and sufficient.

"That's true," Teddy agreed. "*For we walk by faith, not by sight.*"

"A church boy, huh?" Anita nodded as if connecting dots, sizing up who Teddy was as a human being. "That's in Corinthians, right?"

"Yeah, 2 Corinthians 5:7."

"If you meet my mama this weekend, don't tell her I'd forgotten the exact verse."

"Deal," he promised. "Now, tell me more about this food truck in need of repairs."

Anita's dreams and her passion and her hopes resonated strong and clear as she described her vision and talked about the menus she'd created. Her fear of failure and her concerns for getting the business up and running bubbled at the surface as well.

"Let me invest," Teddy offered.

"Nope! Absolutely not—"

"Not as a gift, if you're so determined to push out everyone who wants to help," he interrupted. "Let me *invest*…as a true business partner."

He laid out a proposal, rates and terms far better than what she'd find at a financial institution, but still legitimate enough that Anita didn't perceive the loan as accepting charity.

They negotiated. She fussed; he persisted. Then they jotted the agreed upon details on a napkin that both of them signed. Teddy grabbed his wallet from his backpack and wrote her a check. To his delight, it bore an eye-popping sum with a lot of zeros.

"Baylin's right," Anita said, standing from the booth bench and folding the check before putting it in her back pocket. Her voice carried an earnest note. Her eyes glistened with moisture. "You're not so bad after all."

Teddy would've sworn he'd just received a billion-dollar endorsement.

"Right back at 'cha, partner."

Anita walked away, stopping by tables and exchanging a quick word with other people she knew as she made her way back to the kitchen.

Teddy tenderly shook Baylin's shoulder to wake her up.

"Hey, Sleeping Beauty," he said when she opened her eyes and lifted her head from the pillow of her arms. "If you still want to run to the farm and get back to town for the baseball game, we'd better get going."

"Oh my," she groaned with a stretch. "I think I could call it a night right now and sleep until morning."

"It's your call; you said the high schoolers you hired can handle the booth tonight." A vision of a quiet night by the fireplace in the farmhouse parlor, reading a book from the expansive library, and watching Baylin sew formed in Teddy's mind. The vision held enormous appeal.

"Nah, the Sweetheart Festival comes only once a year. I'd hate to miss a moment of it. Let's get going," she said as they left the restaurant and walked into the chilly winter day. "I'll text Anita to apologize for falling asleep. I'd hate to disrupt her work again."

"She's good," Teddy told her, "…said she'd see you tomorrow at the exhibit hall."

"Oh good. Did y'all get to visit some so you could get to know her? I think she's amazing."

"We did." Teddy opened the driver's door for Baylin. "And you know, I'd say she thinks that same about you."

Baylin gave Teddy a grateful and beautiful smile. Then she pulled her door closed and started the engine while Teddy jogged around to the other side.

They dashed home, checked on animals and water levels, changed clothes, and made it to the baseball field just in time for the "Star-Spangled Banner."

Baylin sat with Teddy in the bleachers for the first three innings. When Chief Everett called her to take right field in the top of the fourth, Teddy walked down the fence line. He cheered and heckled in good fun, enjoying his time as a spectator.

In the bottom of the fifth inning, Teddy clapped and whooped when Baylin hit a line drive between the first and second basemen. Michael Crockett, playing shortstop, wrapped Baylin in a bear hug to prevent her from advancing to third base. Teddy's good mood disappeared.

From where he stood beyond the team bench, he couldn't hear their conversation, but Michael's body language left little for the imagination. His blatant flirtation and excessive hugging struck a nerve that had Teddy seeing red…and not the shade of a sweet Valentine.

Because Michael had interfered with Baylin running the bases, the score was 7–6 going into the sixth and final inning; her team had a one-run lead.

"Can I play?"

"Sorry, son?" the fire chief asked.

Teddy hadn't needed to beg to play ball since kindergarten, but he was fully prepared to do so right then if necessary.

"I'm a friend of Baylin's," he explained. "I'd love to play the last inning, if you're okay with it."

Chief Everett hesitated and squinted to look at Teddy. Either because he'd pulled his cap down low, or because the stadium lights cast a shadow over his features, or because his usual five o'clock shadow had grown into a full-fledged beard the past few days, the older man didn't seem to recognize Teddy.

"I need to win," Chief Everett emphasized. "Stan's won the past two years, and I'm tired of hearing about it every week at Sunday dinner."

"I can help with that, sir."

"Well, alrighty then. Where d'you want to play?"

"I'll take center, if you don't mind." Teddy's legs tingled and his feet itched to get on the field.

"It's all yours."

Teddy jogged out to his position, sad to see someone else had replaced Baylin. Then he heard her cheering from the stands and his heart doubled in size and rhythm. Man, would he like to hear her cheering his name at a Braves game.

The first batter on the other team hit a slow dribbler to second. Teddy could've gotten to the ball and thrown it to first in plenty of time, but he didn't have the heart to throw out the young girl.

The second batter earned a walk.

The third batter popped up to third base…one out, score remained 7–6.

The fourth batter struck out swinging…two outs, still up by one.

The fifth batter happened to be Baylin's admirer, Michael Crockett.

Crockett shouted some good-natured trash talk toward the mound. The pitcher took it in stride, winding up and delivering a pretty decent fastball. Crockett watched it go by. Ball one. On the next pitch, Crockett shifted to swing but halted halfway to watch it go by, too. Ball two. Michael should have the pitcher's speed figured out by the third pitch. He'd likely go yard with it, hitting a home run and putting a win out of reach for Baylin's team.

"Coach, a word?" Teddy called to Chief Everett in the dugout.

"Time, I guess," the umpire called, not hiding his frown nor his frustration at a delay in the game.

"What do you think about me taking the mound?"

The pitcher, who turned out to be Elijah Davis's son and the fireman Baylin told Teddy about, joined their huddle.

"Davis, Baylin's friend here says he'd like to pitch the rest of the inning."

"I bet he would, Chief," Daniel Davis said with a big grin. Then he relented. "We get to watch him play center all the time; let's see if he can pitch, too."

As Davis placed the baseball in Teddy's glove, he teased, "If I was smitten with Baylin O'Casey, I'd want to get rid of Crockett, too."

With no plausible defense, Teddy remained quiet.

"Here we go," Davis hollered in a jaunty voice as he jogged to center field.

The catcher stood to the side of home plate for Teddy to warm up with a few pitches. The disgruntled umpire called everyone back to their places to resume play.

Teddy called time again, gesturing for the catcher to meet him in the infield.

"Good heavens to Betsy," the umpire growled.

"Hi" Teddy said, sounding more awkward than he'd

hoped. "I'm Teddy." He hesitated again. "I should've asked if you've caught before," he said with concern.

"Nice to meet you; I'm Rhys Larsen," the catcher offered, pulling off his catcher's mitt to shake Teddy's hand. "And, uh… I've been catching the entire game."

"I don't mean *here*." Teddy looked around at the high school baseball stadium, at the crowd bundled up under coats and blankets in the stands. His eyes settled on Baylin, who smiled in return.

"I know what you mean, Gwenn."

Teddy looked him right in the eye.

"You won't hurt my hand. Just throw the ball, so we can steal this win right out from under 'em."

Teddy searched Rhys's face for a hint of false bravado but found nothing beyond sheer competitive spirit. Both men nodded at the other in agreement and walked back to their spots behind the plate and on the mound.

After rolling his shoulders and popping his neck, Teddy dragged his front foot across the pitching plate; he didn't even have cleats on.

Why in the world was he making such a big deal of this game?

He played in much bigger venues 162 times a year. Too bad his ego refused to accept reason.

His gaze darted to Baylin, and his determination clicked up yet another notch.

Certain Crockett would watch the first ball for timing, Teddy wound up and released a *fast* fastball. A satisfying snap echoed from Rhys's mitt.

"Woo-wee," someone howled from the stands.

"Strike one," said the umpire.

"Nice pitch," Davis hollered from center field.

Teddy walked back to the mound, fixed the dirt, rocked

back, and fired another fastball — even faster — into Rhys's glove. Crockett had let it go by without swinging again.

"Strike two!"

Teddy scanned the fans as he circled back to the mound a final time. The spectators sat on the edge of their seats, many yelling for one team or the other...a few whispering and pointing in Teddy's direction.

Baylin sat tall, her back ramrod straight. A questioning look had replaced her easy smile.

In for a penny, in for a pound.

Teddy took his place on the mound, smoothed the dirt, pulled the ball and glove to his chest, and released the slowest changeup he'd seen since Little League.

Crockett bit, expecting another fastball and swinging for the fences. He'd swung, missed, and dropped the bat all before the ball had reached Rhys's glove.

"Strike three! Ballgame," the umpire announced. "Everybody outta the cold and on to the Sweetheart Festival."

Cheers erupted from the fire chief's dugout. Grumblings sounded from the police chief's bench. Both coaches and all the players formed two lines to shake hands and offer *Good Games* to one another.

Davis half-jumped on Teddy's back. "Teddy Gwenn, folks... Right here in River City," he hollered with a victorious yell.

Within seconds, a swarm of people surrounded Teddy. He smiled at each one of them, agreed to sign autographs and take pictures, and strove to ignore the dread that had filled his gut like a lead weight.

He looked for Baylin where she'd been sitting, but he didn't find her. The bleacher sat empty.

Baylin was gone.

15

No one goes straight to happiness
after a breakup.
Estelle

"**B**aylin?" Teddy called out.

"Miss O'Casey?" from another voice she didn't recognize.

"Are you in there?" from yet another.

She ignored the shouting and the begging and the caterwauling on her front porch.

"It's our fault," a fourth male whined. "We forced him to hang out with us."

"He's Teddy Gwenn," a pathetic human crowed.

As if I care.

But she did, if for no other reason than to get the infantile mob off her property.

And because Teddy had hurt her.

She'd let herself fall under his larger-than-life spell...let herself believe in love and romance and happy endings.

He'd made a laughingstock of her, and it hurt.

But no one could be as huge an idiot as each of the morons at her door.

It swung open, and Baylin glared daggers at the grown men acting like children in the throes of temper tantrums.

They fell silent, shuffling to attention.

"Are y'all drunk?" she demanded.

"No!" Daniel Davis answered. "We took Teddy to Scooter's for a beer, but that's it. One round. I promise."

"One beer required—" Her words hung in the air as she looked over her shoulder at the grandfather clock in the entry. "…five hours to drink?"

"Only one beer, but many, *many* baseball stories. The old-timers joined in, sharing tales of when the 1962 Wolf Pack won the Oklahoma State Championship—"

"And when the 1980 team—" someone else piped in.

"I don't need a play-by-play." Baylin interrupted.

"Please don't be mad at him," a powerful voice intoned before Max Davenport stepped into the light. "He didn't have much of an option; there's no gracious way to bow out in that situation."

"Of all the people," Baylin said, shaking her head. "Does Janie Lyn know you're out here acting like a fool?"

The professional football player — *living legend,* more like it — chuckled. "Oh yeah," he said in a voice dripping with love for his sweet wife, who Baylin had come to adore through quilt guild meetings and projects. "It's rare I get to be part of a fan club. It was a special night."

"Well, I'm glad it was a banner evening out. What you do is none of my business. That includes Teddy…*except* for the ear-splitting cacophony taking place on my porch." Baylin prayed her words of wisdom sounded more convincing to the men than they did to her own ears. "You're all welcome to continue the party…*in the barn.* Just try not to scare my horses, please."

Baylin nodded and waved good night. She stepped back to close and lock the front door, but Teddy put his hand in the way, forcing her to acknowledge him.

"Can we talk?"

"No."

"Bay—"

"Tomorrow's another long day; I'd like to go to bed."

She looked anywhere except into his eyes. She just couldn't.

It didn't help much. The way he studied her sent cold chills and heat waves across her skin, a physical embodiment of the diametrical tugs on her emotions when she thought of Teddy.

The answer? Don't think about him at all.

"Good night," she said in a tone that could only be described as dismissing.

He got the message and stepped away from the door frame.

Of their own accord, her eyes lifted to his face as she shut the door. The granite set of his jaw and the dark depths of his beautiful green eyes displayed blatant sadness and unveiled concern in their stormy depths.

16

No matter how bad your heart is broken,
the world doesn't stop for your grief.
Faraaz Kazi

After a night of tossing and turning in the barn, Teddy made his way downstairs to fill buckets of grain for the horses at 5:15 a.m., and they already had grain. He entered the chicken coop to gather eggs; either they'd not laid any or someone already collected them. The pigs had empty slop troughs and fresh water. New hay lined the cows' open-front shed.

Did she stay up all night?

Surprised to find it unlocked, Teddy opened the kitchen door with apprehension.

Baylin stood at the sink washing a mug. She looked up when he walked inside, and Teddy had his answer; dark circles under puffy, red-rimmed eyes sent a jagged stab of regret through his gut.

"Good—" he began.

"Jax asked me to tell you that your car is ready," she interrupted.

The knife twisted.

Teddy had spent the week telling Baylin all about Boxy, far beyond anything she'd been interested to hear. He'd shared his worries that the treasured car would never be the same. He'd been on pins and needles waiting for word from the garage.

In that moment, Teddy couldn't have cared less that Jax had finished working on her.

"Oh, that's great." His attempt at enthusiasm flopped.

"I need to leave by seven; if you can be ready by then, I'll drop you off at his shop on my way."

"I'm ready now," Teddy said.

"Great." Her *great* sounded even bleaker than his earlier one.

Teddy opened his mouth to ask how he could help, but she brushed past him.

He couldn't blame her… She felt blindsided.

But at the same time, he'd never lied, never meant to hide who he was. In fact, they'd done nothing but talk as they worked together every minute of the past week. And while the specifics of his upbringing and his job never came up in conversation, Baylin probably knew Teddy and his personality better than anyone else on earth.

"I thought you knew," he called after her.

She halted.

"I told you my name," Teddy added, catching up to her in the hallway. "That first night."

She spun around to face him, anger glowing in her eyes.

"And I should've just known your name?"

"Well, I am kinda famous," he said with an innocent shrug.

That defense failed; her fury escalated.

"Didn't you google me? Isn't that the reasonable thing to do before letting a stranger stay with you?"

"In the barn," she emphasized. "And no, I didn't. You seemed trustworthy. And harmless. You seemed like a good guy."

"I *am* a good guy," he countered.

"Oh no," she said in a voice teetering on hysterical. "I've done my research now…rich and famous, celebrity playboy, a girl at every major league stadium in America!"

"Playboy isn't quite right, and the girlfriend part is a huge exaggeration."

That didn't help the situation, either.

Baylin spun back around, took a step into the pantry, and slammed the door in his face.

Yikes.

He stayed put, leaning against the wall, listening to her shuffle boxes and bins.

When she opened the door to find him there, a frown creased her beautiful face.

"I don't need your help," she informed him, although the crate she carried looked to weigh as much as she did.

"Too bad," he replied, taking the crate from her whether she liked it or not. "You've got it."

They loaded the truck with items to replenish what she'd sold from her booth and drove into town without a word.

"Go straight to the Conrad Hotel," he ordered when she put on her blinker to turn down Main Street toward Jax Fielding's garage. "Please," he tacked on, trying for a gentler tone. Man, could she push his buttons.

Teddy carried the heaviest tubs and crates from the truck to Baylin's booth, but word had spread: *Teddy Gwenn has come to town.* Every few steps, someone stopped to meet him, show him their baseball card collection, ask for an autograph, or take a selfie.

When the expo hall opened to the public, things got exponentially worse.

"Do you mind taking your entourage elsewhere?" Baylin asked, when shoppers couldn't get past his fans to see her displays.

He did as she asked, guiding the group around him to the middle of the exhibit hall, where there was open space.

But he wasn't happy about it.

As a boy, Teddy vowed that if he ever made it to the bigs, he'd always be friendly and kind…no matter how tired he was, no matter the score, and no matter how much he needed to be somewhere else. He'd developed a reputation for being accessible and approachable, arriving early to batting practice and staying late after a game. The people who supported him deserved that. But that day — the *entire* day — the constant flow of people tested his patience. He wanted and needed to be by Baylin's side.

She, too, had a steady stream of people stopping by her booth. Even with two high schoolers there to ring up purchases for her, Baylin worked straight through lunch. He'd kept an eye on her across the room, and she hadn't slowed or sat down at all.

Midafternoon, Teddy extricated himself long enough to visit Anita's setup in the refreshment room.

"How ya doing?" he asked her.

"Better than you, I hear," she answered. "But congratulations on the game last night."

Salt in the wound.

"Yeah," he mumbled. "Thanks."

Anita laughed at him in reply.

"She'll come around," she said.

"You think so?" A twinge of hope tugged at his chest.

"I do," she affirmed. "Baylin's had some tough surprises in her life. Your identity—"

"I never hid—" he interrupted to defend himself. Not defend…explain.

Anita didn't wait to hear his justification.

"Your *full* identity," she continued, speaking over him, "snuck up on her. And if I know Baylin — at least in *her* mind — it proved she shouldn't have risked falling for you."

"But my playing baseball doesn't change how I feel, not about her."

"Maybe not," she said. "But it changes how things progress, how they develop and grow between you. She gave up any ideas she had about leaving Green Hills when she agreed to take on the farm. Your life is the extreme opposite. You might not see that as a roadblock, but Baylin will."

"You think she's falling for me?" he asked with the first genuine smile he'd had since the day before.

"Yes, you big dork. She likes you!" Anita shook her head. "Now buy something… I have this new investor, and he expects a profitable return on his money."

Loaded up with two boxes of assorted pastries and a drink holder full of coffees and teas, Teddy made it through the crowd and back to Baylin's booth without too much hassle. Perhaps that was the trick…don't have hands available for shaking or signing.

She still wouldn't stop to talk to him, but she did say thank you for the coffee, and when she took a sip, Baylin's countenance relaxed, albeit an infinitesimal amount.

Since she wasn't ready to forget or forgive quite yet, Teddy decided he'd find a way to pick up Boxy.

That prospect, paired with Anita's assurance that Baylin would get over being mad at him — *eventually* — put a spring in Teddy's step.

He'd just walked outside and pulled out his phone, hoping to use a ride share app, when a truck pulled up beside him.

Rhys Larsen lowered his window. "Need a lift?" he asked.

"I think so," Teddy answered. "I can't seem to find a car service."

"Not here in Green Hills," Rhys laughed. "Where ya headed?"

"Fielding's Gas & Garage."

"Jax finished with your hot rod?"

"Not a lot of secrets in this town," Teddy replied in lieu of an answer.

"None, to be exact," Rhys laughed. "His garage is on the edge of town; mind if I make a couple of stops along the way? My fiancée handed off her errand list so she could shop at the festival."

"I'm happy to tag along, if you don't mind company." Teddy walked around the the truck and climbed in. "Fiancée, huh? When's the big day?"

"Next month; we leave for Scotland in a couple weeks… feels like I've been waiting all my life to make Maree my wife."

"The fabric designer?" Teddy asked.

"She's the one," Rhys confirmed, adoration heavy in every word and painted all over his face.

"Baylin mentioned her work, said it's incredible."

"Maree's a rare talent," Rhys bragged. "She's also an unbelievable cook."

"Okay," Teddy said with a nod. "That sounds good for you…"

"And for you, too." Rhys insinuated something, but Teddy didn't follow. "Here, take a look…"

He handed over a sheet of paper. Teddy skimmed the list written on it: *two sirloin steaks, one yellow onion, two-pound bag baby potato medley, small sweet potato, spinach, orange bell pepper, yellow squash, 8-ounce sliced Bella mushrooms, medium cucumber, fresh carrots, one pomegranate, pine nuts, three or four apples (assorted types),* and on, and on.

"Looks delicious! Y'all have a special dinner planned?"

"In a manner of speaking," Rhys hedged, pulling into the Get'n'Go parking lot. "Let's get your groceries."

"Excuse me? *My* groceries?" Teddy hustled to catch up to Rhys.

He'd already snagged a basket and selected an onion.

"Did you say *my groceries?*"

"I did," Rhys confirmed.

"Was your offer to give a ride random?"

"*There is no such thing as a coincidence,*" Rhys said with a chuckle.

"Are you quoting *NCIS?*"

"Yep, Gibbs's rule number 9."

"I'm scared that you know the rules *and* the numbers," Teddy commented. His eyebrows wrinkled as he considered that fact, as well as Rhys's admission that he'd been set up.

I'm being set up. On a date.

"What's going on?" Teddy demanded, stepping in the grocery cart's path.

"Word on the street is that you, my friend, are in the doghouse. The Busy Bees' Quilt Guild seems to think you need a helping hand digging out."

"I didn't—"

"Doesn't matter," Rhys interrupted him, pushing the basket around Teddy with a pat on his shoulder. "They have a hunch you're a good thing in Baylin's life, and all they care about is her happiness. Even if nothing comes from your *friendship,*" he hesitated at the word, "…they don't enjoy seeing her sad, not for any reason."

"I want to be a good thing; I want to be in her life," Teddy admitted, deep in thought.

"Maree's going to meet you at Baylin's farmhouse, so she can cook you a dinner to dazzle. Janie Lyn's in charge of getting Baylin home for dinner. Landry — that's Davis's girlfriend and Maree's best friend — is closing up the O'Casey Farm booth tonight. And Miss Sadie's going to soften Baylin's heart a little so she'll be willing to sit through dinner with you."

"I wish you didn't make that last bit sound like the hardest part," Teddy said with chagrin.

"Baylin's got a sweet nature; I'm sure she *wants* to forgive you. But her feelings are hurt, which means her pride is bruised. Sometimes, setting aside our ego is the biggest obstacle."

"I pray this dinner plan works."

"We all are," Rhys said. "I've been there; I almost lost Maree. Take all the help and prayers you can get," he commiserated. "Do whatever it takes to see if she's the one."

"Am I too late for Larsen Love Therapy?" Daniel Davis asked from across the produce department.

"Ha ha," Rhys mocked. "You didn't seem to mind my help last year when you had to convince Landry you were worth taking a chance on love."

"That's a true statement," Davis confessed. "Jax said he tried calling, but neither of you answered. He needs to lock up the shop early. I'm here to steal Teddy and get him over there before Jax closes for the weekend."

Did everyone in Green Hills know his whereabouts and shortcomings?

On one hand, everyone's knowledge and interference in his life startled and disturbed Teddy. On the other hand, he connected with, respected, and appreciated the community's wish to help. He admired the way they wanted to be there for Baylin, and even for Teddy...a virtual stranger.

He thought a lot about that as he drove Boxy to the farm. Teddy decided the pros outweighed the cons. He was all-in with making this dinner a big success for both Baylin and himself.

A win-win.

He couldn't be happy if Baylin wasn't; he couldn't claim a victory if she couldn't, too.

And he had faith.

17

> *God doesn't make mistakes.*
> *Ashli Montgomery*

pple pie out of the oven? *Check.*

Steaks ready for the grill? *Check.*

Salad tossed and chilling in the fridge? *Check.*

Pan-fried veggies over low heat in the skillet? *Check.*

Kitchen table set for two? *Check.*

Candles lit? *Check.*

Teddy consulted the list Maree left for him for the twentieth time. His nerves rattled like a pair of maracas. Beads of sweat popped onto his forehead when her truck rumbled into the garage.

He met her there to help with the empty bins and containers she'd brought home from the festival. He smiled when she paused at the table, studied the vegetables cooking on the range, and returned her gaze to Teddy with a questioning eye.

After they'd unloaded everything, Baylin turned from Teddy and toward the stairs up to her room.

He clutched her wrist before she got away. With a gentle tug, he spun her to face him, just inches away.

"Hi," he said, hoping she couldn't hear his heart beating in his chest louder than a thundering herd.

"Hello," she said. The cautious note in her voice stung, but Teddy forged on.

"I was wondering if you'd like to eat? Here…tonight?" He stumbled, took a deep breath, and tried again. "Please, will you have dinner with me?"

Baylin glanced to the kitchen, then into Teddy's eyes, and moistened her lips, and gave a slight nod. A thread of hope fluttered through his body.

"Give me just a minute," she said, still hesitant, but that was okay.

She'd agreed to spend time with him. *Check.*

When Baylin came down the stairs ten minutes later wearing leggings, an oversized flannel shirt, and big wool socks, Teddy was waiting at the bottom with a bouquet.

"Thank you. These are some of my favorites," she said, holding the flowers close to smell their sweet fragrance.

"Anemones and roses… You talked about them the other day…when we were working in the garden together."

"They're lovely," she said with her first smile, tiny though it was. "Did you get them from the greenhouse?"

"Yes. But full confession," Teddy said, raising his hands in surrender. "Maree Davenport did everything else. And if anything is less than perfect, it's my fault for not successfully following her directions to complete the final touches."

Then Baylin smiled for real. The thread of hope surged into something much more substantial.

"You have great friends," he said. "Nosy and pushy, but great."

Baylin agreed with a song-like laugh. The world looked better and better by the minute.

Teddy smoothed a wave of hair from her face. "You're stunning," he said, taking her hand before she could respond and leading her down the hallway and into the kitchen. "I need to put these steaks on the grill. Maree left strict instructions: five minutes on the first side; flip for three more. I'll be back. Please don't go anywhere."

When he returned exactly eight minutes later, soft music played from the kitchen radio, Baylin had poured two glasses of red wine, and she stood at the sink, looking out toward the barn. Teddy set the steaks on a cool burner, pulled the salad from the fridge, and stirred the vegetable hash for good measure.

"I think we're ready," he said. Baylin turned away from the window to give Teddy her attention. A tear escaped from the corner of her eye. "Please don't cry," he whispered, drying her cheek with his thumb. "I never meant to hurt you. I should've made sure you knew what I do, and what that level of publicity means. Honestly, I convinced myself you already knew, giving myself a pass for not telling you straight. It was selfish... I just *really* enjoyed being plain old me for a few days."

"There's nothing plain or old about you," Baylin said with a small smile and a beautiful blush. "It was a misunderstanding. I'm sorry I made such a big deal about it."

"I'm not." Teddy spoke before Baylin could shrug off the significance. If she didn't care about him more than a little, then she wouldn't have been upset.

"You're glad I flew off the handle, reprimanded your new pals, and gave you a very immature cold shoulder for the past twenty-four hours?"

"I am," Teddy said, with a slight cocky smile. He placed a hand on either side of her waist, pulling her closer. "It means I matter to you. And it brought us here..."

Baylin moistened her lips again. And like when she'd done

it earlier, Teddy had to rein in the desire he felt for her. There was no doubt of their chemistry; they had it in spades.

Their night was about more.

"To dinner," he said, grinning down at her. "Let's eat."

He'd chosen the small kitchen table over the stately dining room table to keep things cozy. He served dinner buffet-style, so the only things between their plates were their wine glasses, two candlesticks, and the salt and pepper shakers...leaving plenty of room to hold hands.

"Do you mind if I bless the food?" Baylin asked before they began eating.

"I'd like that," Teddy answered.

"Dear Lord," she began, bowing her head and closing her eyes. "You don't make mistakes. You brought Teddy to the farm, opened my heart to his staying here, and made me accept his help this week. My life is better and richer for it. Thank you for that. Please guide us, guard us, and keep us safe...wherever we may go. Amen."

"Amen," Teddy echoed.

"Faith was sometimes all we had when I was a kid," Teddy said, cutting into his steak. The only way forward — *together* — was to share his past, a past he didn't talk about often. Not because he was ashamed or because it was tragic, but because it made people feel sorry for him, and he didn't need nor want pity.

The dinner and all the help from Baylin's friends were terrific, but telling his story was the grand gesture. He'd decided it last night, staring at the ceiling in the barn apartment, thinking of Baylin in the wee hours of the night. Letting her in was all he could give, and Teddy was determined to give Baylin — and their future — his all.

While they ate, Teddy described the slums where he grew up, on the wrong side of the tracks in a small town outside Baton Rouge, Louisiana. He told her about his parents, who loved him the best they could, but worked way too much for far too little and had little left for a rambunctious son.

Baylin seemed to enjoy his tales of playing street ball with the neighborhood kids every possible moment of the day, and even in the night when they found a park or field with lights. And she laughed outright when he imitated how he'd pronounced his name as a little boy, "Ted G'win, as in, Ted gonna win it all!"

He pointed out good things, too, careful not to paint a one-sided picture of a latchkey kid living a depressing existence on the poor side of town, even if that was most accurate.

"Baseball was your ticket out," Baylin said.

"And I never looked back."

"What about your family?"

"They're good…better, at least. My first Major League contract got them out of debt and into decent housing. They're proud; it's a struggle to get them to take what I'd like for them to have. But they let me help support the boys, my two younger brothers." Teddy smiled, thinking of the two hellions.

"Do they play baseball, too?"

"Oh, yeah. Dad loves baseball. We're all named for legends of the game. He had us catching a ball by the time we could run, so I guess we never had a choice. But even if we would've had one, we'd have played. Our bats and gloves might've been cheap and second-hand, but we didn't care."

"Are your brothers as good at baseball as you?"

"Promise not to tell?"

"My lips are sealed," she pledged with a zipped-lip gesture.

"I think they're even better."

"Where do they play now?"

"They're a lot younger than I am; Lou is sixteen, and Mickey's only twelve."

"Because of your success, poverty hasn't shaped them in the same way it affected you."

Teddy shrugged; he was no saint or savior.

"Do you see them?"

"Not as much as I should. They come to a few games during the summers, and I try to make a few of theirs around my schedule. I could do a much better job of getting back to visit."

"What makes it difficult to go?"

"I want to fix everything for Mom and Dad. I could if they'd let me." He'd had the argument with his parents enough times to hear it play out in his mind, so even telling Baylin about it brought his frustrations to the forefront. "If they'd just choose to be happy, attempt to enjoy life. A new approach can do wonders."

"That explains your unceasing determination to be cheerful."

Was that a compliment or an insult?

Teddy examined Baylin's expression, looking for signs of derision. He couldn't find any.

Still, her insightfulness made him uncomfortable.

He stood from the table, cleared their empty plates, and refilled their wineglasses.

They worked in quiet tandem to put away the leftover food and load their plates and silverware into the dishwasher. He rolled up his sleeves to wash the pots and pans, and Baylin dried them.

When they'd finished cleaning up from dinner, Baylin led the way to the parlor.

Teddy followed her, carrying their drinks, the apple pie Maree had made, two plates, and two forks, which he arranged on the coffee table. Then he added wood to the fireplace and lit a fire.

Baylin settled on the couch, patting the cushion beside her for him to sit there.

Such a small gesture, yet it caused his heart to skip a beat. Perhaps his grand gesture would work…he prayed it would draw her nearer rather than push her away.

"My happiness isn't fake," he explained. "I love my life. It's not as easy as the television makes it seem; I have to work on my game, my speed in the outfield, and my hitting all the time. Otherwise, I'll lose my spot to one of the hundred — more like *thousands* — of guys who'd love a shot at it."

"That's why you've been working out in the barn."

His head snapped up to meet her gaze. He'd been running the stairs, from the lower level of the barn to his condo and back down for forty-five minutes, pushing tractor tires across the open space, and logging five hundred sit-ups and one hundred pull-ups before they started farm chores each morning. He hadn't realized she knew.

"I came in to feed the horses Monday and saw you," she said.

"Did you now?" Teddy questioned, enjoying the way her cheeks burned at her memory of him shirtless in her barn. "Do tell."

"Yes, well… I didn't want to disturb you, so I *immediately* walked out."

"Sure, you did," he teased, tickling her as he gave her a hard time.

"I did!" She protested around her giggles. Then she tried tickling him back, which turned into wrestling on the couch. And since Teddy was bigger and stronger, the wrestling ended up with Baylin pinned and panting underneath him, eyes glossy and glistening with laughter, and Teddy way too close to losing control.

He tickled her ribs one last time to make her squirm, and then Teddy lifted himself off Baylin and went to tend the fire…the one burning just fine of its own accord.

Fine, Lord. Call me a coward. I'm a coward. I admit it…a weak, falling in love, goofy old fool.

"Is this week the longest you've gone without practicing?" Baylin asked. "Minus the game last night, which I'm guessing wasn't much of a practice for you." Her smarty-pants expression said it all. Busted.

"Nah, I guess it wasn't," he admitted. "But that guy got in my head… I wanted to beat him so bad that my nerves went a little wild."

"Who? Michael?"

"That's the one. I hated seeing him flirt with you on the field. I just lost it…saw red, the whole enchilada."

He'd sat back down on the couch next to where Baylin sat facing him, criss-cross style. Teddy glanced at her, embarrassed by his behavior the night before.

She shook her head and laughed before putting his worries to rest.

"I told you: I've known Michael — and his entire family — my whole life. He's just a friend. That's all he's ever been, and that's all he'll ever be."

Teddy nodded, accepting Baylin at her word.

"It was quite entertaining to see your Bruce Banner slash Incredible Hulk transformation," she said, poking him in the ribs.

"I can't believe I let him get to me," Teddy groaned, covering his face with both hands. "I mean, that's why I choose joy… I choose to live in the moment because it keeps the wolves at bay."

"On that we can agree," Baylin said, unfolding her legs and moving forward on the cushion to reach the apple pie. She sliced it, putting a quarter of the pie on his plate and a smaller sliver on her own. Then she scooted to rest her back against the arm of the couch, still facing Teddy. He did the same on the opposite end.

"Growing up, I'd always planned on going to college for a business degree. I wanted to own my own flower shop back here in Green Hills someday. I had travel journals lined out for all the places I'd go first, though…so I could bring back the inspiration of the most magnificent flowers in the world. Everything crumbled my senior year. Just a few days before graduation, my grandpa died. He had an accident on the farm, doing a task he'd done a million or more times. In the aftermath of his sudden death, we realized my grandma's struggles with memory loss were much more than mere forgetfulness. With Papa Joe gone, she declined faster than we could have imagined. By the end of that summer, we moved her into Memorial Care, the memory care facility in town. Being at home had turned unsafe for her. Taking her there broke my heart."

"Is she still living?" Teddy asked, taking a napkin from under the pie plate and handing it to Baylin for her tears.

"No," she said, wiping her eyes. "She didn't make it a full year after that." She sniffled, dried her cheeks, and squared her shoulders, fortifying her brave front. "My parents had no interest in staying here; they'd never loved the farm or Green Hills the way Papa Joe did, the way I do. They wanted to sell the farm, pay off the debts, and put the rest of the funds in an account for my college expenses."

"That sounds reasonable, so you could pursue your own life and dreams."

"It does, and that was their argument. But I just couldn't do it… I couldn't walk away from our family's legacy, the place I love more than any other on earth. I convinced them to let me try my hand at running the farm. We agreed to a five-year deal. At the end of the five years, I'll have paid them for their share of the farm."

"When does the lease expire?"

"August thirty-first…on my twenty-fifth birthday."

"And that's why finances are so tight around here? Because you're paying off the lease in just five years?"

She nodded *yes,* taking a bite of her dessert.

"That's quite an accomplishment," Teddy said, impressed.

"Things *have* been tight," she admitted before taking a sip of her wine. "But it's been good for me. I had to be diligent, watch every penny, and weigh every decision."

"Since I'm paying *five hundred dollars* a night to sleep with the horses, I'd say you've taught yourself well."

She grinned at his ribbing.

"College helped; I had no clue how little I knew when I assumed responsibility for the farm. And I've had guidance and support from friends in the community."

"Did you take classes online?"

"Yes, some friends from high school went to Tarleton State University in Texas, on rodeo scholarships. They told me all about the school before we graduated, so I knew it was an exceptional school for agriculture. I'd planned on Southern Methodist University in Dallas, where my mom and dad met, but I needed to switch degrees to Ag Business rather than Entrepreneurship. Tarleton offered the program I needed in a remote learning format and a late admissions process, so I wouldn't have to sit out a year. I started on time that fall and graduated with my Bachelor of Science in Agribusiness four years later."

"That's an incredible journey," Teddy said, even more impressed.

"Yeah, not the journey I envisioned in the beginning, but one I've loved."

"Where were you planning to travel? To see the flowers?"

"Oh, wow! Let's see..." A dreamy look drifted across Baylin's face. "The Chelsea Flower Show, for sure. The lavender fields in Provence, France. I'd have toured galleries to see Monet's *Water Lilies,* van Gogh's sunflowers, and Georgia O'Keefe's signature flowers. And those would've been a drop in the bucket of what was on my list."

"You and those lists," he teased. "Will you still go?"

"Maybe," she answered, her expression one of mixed emotions. "I'd still like to have that flower shop in town someday; between weddings, funerals, holidays, and special events, Green Hills needs another one to keep up with demand. But the farm comes first, and I'm happy keeping my focus on it."

She set her empty dessert plate on the table, swallowed the last sip of her wine, and pulled a quilt from a stack folded under the coffee table. Teddy carried the pie, their dishes, and the wine glasses to the kitchen. He stopped by the restroom, added one more log to the fire, and rejoined Baylin on the couch.

Instead of leaning against the arm, she curled up in the center.

"You can take off your shoes, ya know?"

The small nicety felt like a big invitation.

And when he got situated next to her, she fluffed the quilt to cover them both.

"Hang on," Teddy said, leaning forward to take off the heavy sweater he'd worn all day.

"Another baseball shirt?" she teased when she saw the tee he wore under the sweater.

"When I got to college, the school gave us clothes. Lots of clothes! And not just baseball clothes, but extra shoes, joggers, shorts, t-shirts, sweatshirts, socks...even underwear. It was amazing. It's all I wore. I mean, why spend money if I didn't have to, right?"

"Where'd you go to school?"

"Louisiana State."

"LSU Tigers," she said. "Didn't you tire of wearing purple and gold every moment of every day?"

"Nope. Best of all, when I got to the minors, I got a whole new wardrobe."

Teddy told Baylin about being drafted by the Braves in the 2017 Major League Baseball Draft, pick number 457. He walked her through his minor league career, describing each mascot so she'd know which t-shirt went with which team. He shared his elation at being called up to the big league in 2019, and he even mentioned the record he set for most stolen bases by a rookie.

They talked for hours. She never mentioned him going to the barn. Teddy never asked.

He noticed well past midnight that Baylin had drifted off to sleep leaning against him.

Teddy shifted her in his arms, imprinting the feeling of her snuggled in his embrace on his memory so he would remember it forever. His breathing fell into sync with hers, and eventually, he joined her in sleep.

The sun, bright through the large parlor windows, woke Teddy first.

Their fire died during the night, but wrapped in one another's arms under the blanket, they stayed cozy and warm. He had, however, lost feeling in one arm.

He adjusted her weight to be more fully on his chest so the blood would return to his fingers and hand. The jostling woke her…the exact opposite of what he'd been trying to do.

"Good morning," she whispered, rubbing her face against his chest like a kitten burrowing for comfort.

"Good morning," he said through a smile he couldn't contain.

"Sorry I fell asleep on you—"

"I'm not," he interjected.

"I believe we were up to 1957, when Porsche stopped making your car."

"Boxy," he reminded her.

"Believe me, I could never forget…named that because all ninety of the Porsche 550 models ever made achieved unprecedented success on the racing circuit, where Formula One racers hear or call *box* when they need to return home."

"And because…" Teddy prompted.

"You're highly successful in the batter's box."

"You were listening," he praised, squeezing her tight until she giggled.

"I was listening," she affirmed, snuggling even closer. "All seventy-five times you've told me."

Teddy moved his hand over her ribs, threatening to tickle her for exaggerating so dramatically, but he switched gears instead.

"Wanna take a ride in Boxy?" he asked.

"Me?"

"I'm pretty sure we're the only two people in this room, on this couch, and under this quilt."

She giggled again.

"You mentioned having faith last night," she said instead of answering. "Would you go to church with me this morning?"

"Absolutely."

"Afterward, I need to run by the booth, make sure the kids will take it all down when the festival ends this afternoon."

"Sounds good."

"So maybe we could go for a ride together after that?"

"Perfect!"

18

___

"So This is Love"
Song lyrics written by
Al Hoffman, Mack David,
and Jerry Livingston
and performed by Ilene Woods
and Mike Douglas
in Walt Disney's Cinderella (1948)

"You seem to have settled your differences," Janie Lyn Davenport said, joining Baylin after church.

"Well, the differences are still there, but the misunderstanding over them seems less daunting today," Baylin told her. "At least I hope so. I don't want to lose him, but I'm scared I will in the end."

"Anything I can do to help? I might have some insight into the concerns I'm sure you have over his career."

Baylin looked across the churchyard to where every boy from church — young and old — huddled around Max Davenport and Teddy Gwenn.

"You'd think they'd never seen a professional athlete," Baylin joked.

"Maxwell is thrilled to have Teddy here…moves some of the spotlight onto someone else," Janie Lyn confided.

"Is it difficult?" Baylin asked. "Being with a celebrity football player?"

"It isn't always easy," Janie Lyn answered. "I don't imagine any relationship is, regardless of what careers those involved pursue."

"It just seems like the travel and the schedule and the lifestyle add additional layers of challenges."

"I'm sure they do for some couples. Maxwell and I face life head on. Whether handling the uniqueness of his career, my family history — which, as you know, is another issue entirely — or anything else that arises, we lean on one another, and we always put *us* first."

"What about all the time he's away?"

"Football differs from baseball in that they play fewer games, but I'd guess that between training camps, meetings, preseason, the regular season, and postseason opportunities, the time commitments are similar."

"Is he ever home?"

Janie Lyn chuckled. "Home *base* is Green Hills. *Home* is wherever we are together. I attend as many games as I can around the projects I have going with The Christmas Collection project here. And when the strain of being apart gets heavy, I travel to be with Maxwell."

"I'm not sure I can do that with the farm."

"It's not the same situation, that's true," Janie Lyn allowed. Sympathy filled her kind eyes. "Henry Ford said, *Obstacles are those frightful things you see when you take your eyes off your goal.* Conversely, if you look for solutions, you and Teddy will find them. If you love one another, then building a life together —

however that looks with Green Hills as a home base and intentional planning around his baseball schedule to spend time together — is worth whatever it takes to follow your hearts."

If you love one another…

Did they?

Baylin snuck another glance Teddy's way. Their eyes met. That had happened all morning, all throughout church.

When their hands had touched during the service, their fingers entwined. Neither pulled away.

They'd only known each other a few days; they'd only confirmed their feelings toward one another hours before.

Did Cupid always work so fast?

A litany of questions ricocheted around her brain.

Am I merely a conquest Teddy wants to win?

He'd made it no secret that he didn't like to lose. And he'd been adamant that she change the way she lived. Was the attraction between them just another game?

Despite the doubts creeping into her subconscious, Baylin's heart yearned to try, yearned to love.

Belief that Teddy felt the same way dominated her considerations. And weren't belief and faith one and the same?

Mr. Mitchell's sermon that morning had focused on faith.

He began the lesson with a quote attributed to Bill Gates, *With great wealth comes great responsibility.*

Then he shared a photo of the 1962 *Amazing Fantasy #15* edition of Stan Lee's *Spider Man* comic book, which said the same thing: *With great power comes great responsibility.*

Next, Mr. Mitchell had asked everyone to turn to Luke 12:47–48…

The servant who knows the master's will and does not get ready or does not do what the master wants will be beaten with many blows. But the one who does not know and does things deserving punishment will be beaten with few blows. From everyone who has been given much, much will be demanded; and from the one who has been entrusted with much, much more will be asked.

And to read Matthew 21:22…

And whatever you ask in prayer, you will receive, if you have faith.

Mr. Mitchell challenged the congregation to connect the two concepts to each individual's personal life experiences. First, by listing three types of wealth present in one's life. His examples included health, happiness, and success. Baylin had written *the farm, family legacy,* and *personal relationships.*

The second step was to list the responsibilities that came with each type of wealth written on the paper. Duties and chores never strayed far from Baylin's mind; she didn't have to think long about her answer…*caring for the animals, caring for the land, caring for my loved ones.*

For the third and final step, Mr. Mitchell instructed everyone to think about how the three types of wealth were obtained and how prayer and faith played a role in receiving the blessings of that wealth.

I'd have nothing without God's help; I've prayed for each of these gifts time and time again, and the Lord provided. I have faith that my prayers will come true.

Baylin circled what she'd written and drew a large star beside it.

Receiving Teddy's love would be the richest of gifts. Possessing such a treasure meant accepting the great responsibility of having faith in his love, in their devotion to one another. That, in turn, required belief they would always find a way forward, a way in which they *both* won. Thus, winning and trusting Teddy with her heart were the same.

I love Teddy Gwenn.

"*I*'m ready to go," Baylin said. Well, she mouthed it more than said it, since the fan club around Teddy and Max had increased rather than decreased.

He smiled, nodded, and waved in every direction, weaving his way through the masses and to Baylin's side.

"I'm ready to go," she repeated. "On that car ride."

"What about your booth?"

"After church dismissed, I spoke to one of the high schoolers helping me this weekend. I gave him the key to the cargo trailer. After the kids load what's left at the booth, he'll pull it to the farm and leave the key in the barn. I'm free for the rest of the day."

Had she *ever* said those words in her life?

"What about the farm?"

"I hired someone to feed, water, and check lines this evening. Everything else can wait until tomorrow."

She'd *never* uttered those words!

"But what about your quilt? I thought the final festival event was an assembly to announce the winners of all the competitions."

"I've already won."

"You won? That's amazing. I knew—"

"No, no, no." Baylin waved her hands to get Teddy's attention. "I didn't win the contest— I mean, I don't know who placed in all the different categories. It doesn't matter."

"It doesn't?"

"No, I won a greater prize," she said, sidling up to Teddy with a grin.

"Did you now?"

Baylin didn't need a mirror to know her cheeks turned the color of a firetruck…just as they had when he'd said that same thing in that same way the night before, when she'd admitted to seeing him half-dressed in her barn. *He* didn't need to know it had happened more than once. On purpose.

"Yes, I'll tell you all about it," she said in her best impression of someone who knew how to flirt. "When we're on the road…with Boxy."

That did it. Teddy hollered a generic farewell and grabbed Baylin's hand to drag her to the truck.

Going all caveman turned out to be unnecessary; Baylin matched him stride for stride.

"*This* is the seatbelt? This harness…thingy? Good heavens, is it even legal?"

"Baylin, it's a vintage race car," Teddy pointed out with his signature boy-like charm. Unnecessarily, of course. After a week of Teddy's endless Boxy talk, Baylin could've described every stitch of the tan vinyl basket-weave interior, listed every element of the aluminum 4-cylinder engine, and recited every part of the two sandcasted carburetors and dual ignition.

"Yes, I'm aware," she muttered.

"Come on, Bay; strap in…"

Teddy's voice — normally so boisterous — held a near-serious thread of imploring hope. Baylin held his heart in the palm of her hands; she held their future in her next move.

Such power both invigorated and humbled Baylin.

As did his patience…his unrelenting faith.

Teddy gave her time. He gave her space to make her decision, *their decision.*

Where did the road lead from there?

Teddy ran the back of his fingers down her cheek before brushing the pad of his thumb across her bottom lip. Studied adoration intensified the crystal depths of his leafy green eyes.

Tongue-tied, Baylin searched for traces of doubt, of signs they could fail. She found none.

"It's Valentine's Day… Will you be mine?" he asked.

She nodded, placing her heart and her trust into his hands just as he'd gifted his to her.

Then she settled into her seat, pulled the harness straps over each shoulder, and fastened the clasp at her waist, ready to merge two individual paths into one they'd traverse together.

Baylin tightened the straps to fit her frame, metaphorically securing their hopes and dreams in the process. She wiggled in the seat to test the mechanism.

Snug as a bug in a rug.

Baylin lifted her gaze to find Teddy brimming with elation and straining to contain his joy. It filled the tiny space of the car's cockpit.

A blanket of warmth rippled through Baylin's nerves and expanded throughout her chest and lungs and heart. That feeling of wonder did little to calm the rapid beating of her pulse. Nervous excitement forced a giggle she couldn't suppress.

So this is love.

Not yet held in place by his seat harness, Teddy swooped in to steal a kiss.

What might've been a sweet little peck escalated into a passionate declaration of love and promise and devotion.

"Ready?" Teddy whispered against Baylin's lips.

"For?" she whispered right back.

"We're swinging for the fences," he pledged. "It'll be the ride of our lives."

"In that case, let's go," Baylin challenged, wrapping a hand around the back of his neck and pulling his lips to hers for one more kiss, one to seal the deal…one to declare them both victorious, both winners in the game of love.

**...*to the victor belong the spoils of the enemy.*
New York Senator William H. Marcy,
*January 1832***

he End.

BOOK 6 PLAYLIST

There are more love songs than anything else.
If songs could make you do something
we'd all love one another.
Frank Zappa

Enjoy the music that helped inspire the story…

1. Earth Angel - The Penguins
2. L-O-V-E - Nat King Cole
3. Chasing After You - Ryan Hurd & Maren Morris
4. The Lady in Red - Chris de Burgh
5. Belong Together - Mark Ambor
6. Until I Found You - Stephen Sanchez & Em Beilhold
7. This Year's Love - David Gray
8. How Long Will I Love You - Ellie Goulding
9. Baby Can I Hold You - Tracy Chapman
10. This is How You Fall in Love - Jeremy Zucker & Chelsea Cutler
11. It's in His Kiss - Betty Everett

12. Kiss - Vitamin String Quartet
13. Kiss - Dean Martin
14. Pause - Pit Bull
15. Pause - Amelia Day
16. Pause. Breathe. - Kindred Worship
17. Be Still - The Fray
18. Let's Be Still - The Head and The Heart
19. Happy - Kyle Hume
20. Made to Love - Toby Mac
21. Love is Here - Tenth Avenue North
22. This Will Be (An Everlasting Love) - Natalie Cole

———

Available on Spotify as
"Book 6: Stealing Kisses
by Virginia'dele Smith"

ABOUT THE AUTHOR

Ashli Montgomery is a wife, a momma, a writer, a quilter, and an entrepreneur. Her passion is sharing love stories, books, quilts, yoga, recipes, and her favorite ways to create a lovely life.

Ashli writes wholesome and cozy romance under the pen name *Virginia'dele Smith* to honor Syble Virginia Tidwell, Adele Gertrude Baylin, and Etta Jean Smith.

These three cherished grandmothers taught Ashli to love without judgment, always putting family first. Through Grandma Syble's journals and appetite for books, through Momadele's priceless cards and handwritten letters, and through hours of visiting over fabric at Mema's kitchen island, Ashli also learned to treasure words.

Get to know Ashli by subscribing to her newsletter, *The Gazette*, at AshliMontgomery.com

Titles by Virginia'dele Smith

Sadie & Sam: PART 1 - Introductory Short Story (FREE)
Book 0: My Manifesto - Short Memoir (FREE)

The Davenports
Book 1: Grocery Girl
Book 2: In the Trenches
Book 3: Three Times to Make Sure
Book 4: Take a Chance on Love
The Davenports EAT — A Green Hills Cookbook

Book 5: Undeveloped Love
A Christmas Collection Novella

Book 6: Stealing Kisses
A Valentine's Sweetheart Story

Book 7: Phoebe (Coming Soon)
The Prairie Roses Collection

Ashli not only writes about quilts, quilters, and quilting… She's a quilter, too!

When she's not writing, Ashli is often helping others complete their quilt projects through her longarm sewing business, Longarm Lucey, and _quilting to mend the mind_ by connecting quilters with the fight to end Alzheimer's disease through Quilt 2 End ALZ, Inc., a 501(c)(3) nonprofit she launched in 2019, to use her quilting hobby as a platform to advocate for a world without Alzheimer's disease and other forms of dementia.

Learn more at Quilt2EndALZ.org

9 781957 036243